Cole reluctantly sat across from Agnieszka. He was immediately entranced by her brown eyes, which seemed to look past his skin and into the depths of his consciousness. He found her to be confounding, to be sure, and yet equally bewitching. Cole briefly thought that in a completely different situation, he might have fallen in love with this woman.

"Well?" he asked.

"Ask me the question that is on your mind."

"Am I dead?"

She studied him for a moment and then gently answered, "Yes, you are."

Cole felt a stab of sorrow in his chest, for he knew she spoke the truth. He had been in denial ever since he'd "awoken" from being murdered. Although he didn't understand what was happening to him now, Cole accepted that this was indeed his fate.

"I am, too, by the way," Agnieszka said. "Have you noticed that no one here can see me either?"

Cole looked around at all the party revelers. None of them looked their way.

"You're right. Why is it that they usually don't see or hear me, but then sometimes they can?"

"Because you can appear to the living when you want to. There's a…trick to it. You have to learn how to do it."

"And how do I do that?"

"You have seen movies and read books about ghosts, am I right? Throughout history, people have spoken about 'seeing a ghost' and sometimes even talking to one. One minute the ghost is there, and then it is gone. You can do that. It takes practice, but once you figure out the method, you will be able to do it."

HOTEL DESTINY

A Ghost Noir

by Raymond Benson

FOR THE GHOSTS OF MY ANCESTORS

ACKNOWLEDGMENTS

The author wishes to thank John Everson and Brian Pinkerton for their wise comments on this manuscript, and David N. Wilson and David Dodd at Crossroad Press. Much love and gratitude go to my agent, Cynthia Manson, and to my best critic and supporter, Randi Frank.

FROM
THE *NEW YORK DAILY HERALD*
OCTOBER 31, 1985

HOTEL DESTINY

GRAND RE-OPENING TONIGHT

After years of operating as a transient and often controversial landmark near Times Square in Manhattan, the twelve-story Hotel Destiny is set to re-open in grand style on Halloween night with a costume party that new owner and manager Marvin Trent claims will, "recall the glory days of the early twentieth century."

The hotel has a checkered history. The first owner/manager was Laurence Flynn, whose wife Theresa was involved in a murder/suicide with silent film star Bradley Granger. The incident happened during a similar grand opening costume party on Halloween night of 1917. The hotel flourished despite the scandal, and for its first decade it was a top-class destination for visitors and New York elite.

The Great Depression took a toll, however, and after Flynn's own mysterious death in 1931, the hotel experienced a serious decline in stature in the 1930s and '40s. The place became a haven for characters associated with organized crime, namely alleged mobster James "Curly" Chadwick, until a fire—attributed to arson—demolished a floor of living quarters in July of 1948. Miranda Flynn, daughter of Laurence Flynn and owner of the property at the time, perished in the catastrophe.

Colorful real estate magnate J. T. Dunlap bought the building, repaired most of the damage, and re-opened Hotel Destiny in 1951 as an inexpensive and—some say—eyesore establishment in the heart of the theatre district, attracting the more unsavory elements associated with the Times Square area for three decades.

Five unsolved murders occurred in the building over the years since 1972, the victims being a maid employed at the hotel and guests living on society's fringes. The most recent offense was committed earlier this year, on Valentine's Day, when purported call-girl Martine Crawford was found shot to death in one of the guest rooms. Police investigators have said that the crimes might be the work of a single serial killer.

Developer Trent vowed to change the hotel's reputation when he purchased the building in 1983 from Dunlap's estate and began a remodeling that would restore Hotel Destiny to the original look and feel of the 1917 edition. The lobby, ballroom, and the rooms have been completed. The kitchen has been updated with modern appliances, but there are still administrative offices that need to undergo a facelift.

Despite the recent killing, Trent has proclaimed that the new "old" Hotel Destiny will be luxurious, affordable, and above all, safe.

When asked, due to the many deaths and murders that have transpired there, if the hotel is haunted, Trent laughs and answers, "I hope so! That will add to its mystique!"

1

He had been the night manager and self-proclaimed hotel detective since 1974.

A fat lot of good he did, though. Not counting the slain maid found in the boiler room in 1972, which was before his time at the hotel, four more murders had occurred on his watch. He had been powerless to prevent them, and he had been equally inept in helping the police solve the crimes. Three women and one man had taken bullets to their heads in 1976, 1978, 1982, and earlier this year, in 1985. All most likely from the same gun and same killer.

That did not look good on the resume of someone who was supposed to be head of security.

Coleman Sackler stood in his dumpy office, stared at his reflection in the mirror on the wall near the door, and fondled the stubble on his weather-beaten face. He was thirty-seven going on fifty. His normally black hair was already turning gray on the sides. The bags under his eyes and the crow's feet at the corners betrayed a life of sleeplessness and too much booze. Sometimes, when there was nothing to do, he'd gaze out the one window behind his cluttered desk and count the bricks in the back of the building behind the hotel. If he stood at the side of the window and peered at a clumsy angle to the east, he could see a sliver of Seventh Avenue. When that became too boring, he would stand and look at himself in the mirror, wondering how his life had taken him to this spot.

He didn't believe in what they called "depression." Cole figured that he was simply a cranky misanthrope. Always had been, always would be.

This trait kind of made him the perfect bouncer for a hotel when that duty was required of him.

The office was situated in the conglomeration of small rooms that were positioned behind the reception desk on the ground floor. If he were needed, a concierge—when the hotel employed one—or a receptionist could slap one of those old-fashioned bells that sat on the counter, and he would come running. Just go out the door of his office, down a corridor of thirty feet, through an archway, and he was at the front desk. How many times had he been called out to deal with the New York Street Skunk—the bums, drunks, addicts, hookers and their johns, gangbangers, and other unwanted humanity from the New York City streets who had wandered into the lobby over the eleven years of his tenure? Too many to count, that was for sure. Cole was an imposing six-foot, two inches of ex-army cannonball, although in the time since his deployment in Nam he had let a lot of the muscle go to hell. Still—one look at him, and most of the time the riff raff would turn around and skedaddle. There were several instances in which he had had to pull the strong arm to throw someone out the door, and quite a few times when he'd had to call the cops. He never liked phoning the police. It made him feel inadequate. Sergeant Redenius of the 14th Precinct was a stand-up guy, but Cole had the feeling the man thought the Hotel Destiny's night manager was an alcoholic screw-up.

In truth, Redenius wasn't wrong, and Cole knew it.

When had it all gone into the toilet? It wasn't when the IRS had told him that he owed an obscene amount of money in back taxes. It wasn't when Janine kicked him out of their apartment in Brooklyn and divorced him, forcing him to live at the hotel for the past two years. Cole had taken over the adjoining office and made it his bedroom, and he liked that just fine. He couldn't blame Janine. She had fallen in love with another man, someone with a good job and better character. A guy who didn't drink, even though *she* did.

No, the downturn had to have been before Vietnam. His school years had been awful, especially prior to the growth spurt and he began to tower over the bullies, but he had overcome all that, eventually graduated from high school, and became a man.

The burn scars on his left leg, hip, and side that he'd had

since he was too young to remember were not the source of his problems either. He'd lived with the grafted skin patches his entire life. No big deal.

Maybe it was when he'd experienced his first Dream State at the age of five. It was sort of a "waking dream," or really just an intense daydream. This curious condition was something that had occurred to Cole a few times when he was a child, less as a teen, and then he'd mostly grown out of it. He'd dubbed it the Dream State. What would happen was that he'd simply be doing something one minute, and then he'd start to daydream about a memory. An event in his past. He'd lose himself in it, and it seemed so real that he'd think he was re-living it. The next thing he knew he was lying down somewhere with his adoptive mom or dad fussing over him. His parents didn't know what to make of that, and neither did the several doctors who had attempted to diagnose him. These "blackouts," as *they* called them, happened less frequently as he got older, but the phenomenon occasionally—but rarely—still occurred in his adult years when he least expected it. Luckily, he'd been able to hide this talent from the army and his employer. Cole genuinely enjoyed Dream States when they took place, and he sometimes wished he could bring them on at will. Back then, though, the anxiety they caused his parents made him think something was terribly wrong with his head.

He wondered if Charlie—if Charlie was real—got them. Charlie. The imaginary brother, as his mother used to call him. She had once told Cole that when he was very young, he would pretend to have a brother during play. Cole didn't remember that at all, but he did recall several instances as an older child and later as an adult when, during a Dream State, Cole had a feeling that he *did* have a brother and could often feel his presence. Sometimes he had a conversation with him. It was not a pleasant sensation. Cole had named this phantom sibling Charlie. Since Cole had been adopted from an orphanage, he supposed it was *possible* there was a brother, but his adoptive parents never said this was the case, if they even knew. Cole figured he had an overactive imagination and it was just a weird fantasy he'd had since he was a kid.

Turning away from the mirror, Cole surveyed the office. The place looked exactly as it did when the hotel first opened in 1917, just dirtier and aged. The offices were the part of the hotel that had not yet been refurbished. His new boss, Marvin Trent, had declared that the guests came first. He started the project by renovating all the rooms, then the kitchen, and finally all the common areas—the elevators, the lobby and stairs, the ballroom, and the dining room. The improvements had done wonders for what had been a fleabag, miserable dump of a Times Square hellhole for nearly three decades. Now it was damn-near glamorous.

Trent had bought the place two years earlier and it had taken that long to revamp all twelve floors. They would finally get to the offices, storage areas, and other rooms unseen by the public in early 1986. Cole couldn't wait for a workspace that didn't smell like mold and decades-old dust. It would certainly make his job easier to take. That is, if he continued to still be employed. He never knew when Trent was going to give him the axe. The real estate mogul and hotelier was not happy with Cole, especially after the body of that hooker was found in Room 605 in February.

Maybe things would get better. A completely different type of clientele would stay at Hotel Destiny from now on. First, though, there was the grand re-opening goddamn costume party that had to be survived, and it was that evening.

To hell with it….

Cole went around the decades-old desk, opened the top left drawer, and removed the Smith & Wesson Model 10-5 38 Special revolver that he'd kept in there forever in case he needed it.

Is it time? Is it finally time?

To give himself the courage, he also took hold of the pint of Jack Daniel's, opened it, and swallowed a long, burning swig. He gasped and coughed and winced, replaced the cap, and stuck the bottle back in the drawer.

Cole then held the gun in his right hand, went across the faded Parisian rug back to the mirror, and looked into his bloodshot eyes. He raised the weapon high, pointed the barrel at his right temple, and, without hesitation, squeezed the trigger.

Click.

He emitted a short, guttural laugh. Of course the damned thing was empty! He was such a loser that he had forgotten to load the cylinder chambers after cleaning it the night before.

Hey, you know what might be interesting? What was that movie with Robert De Niro and Christopher Walken that came out a few years ago? The one in Vietnam. Where the Viet Cong made them play…

…Russian Roulette!

Cole went back to the desk, found the box of cartridges, and slipped only one into a single chamber. He made sure all the other slots were empty, spun the cylinder like they did in the western movies, spun it again for luck, and flicked it closed.

He went back to the mirror, looked at himself, and noticed that there were now tears in his eyes. Where had *those* come from? He didn't know and didn't care.

Cole raised the pistol to his head, the barrel against his temple. Finger on the trigger.

Was there a bullet in the chamber?

Was this the end of Coleman Sackler?

Only one way to find out.

He squeezed the trigger.

Click.

RRRRRRRIIIIINGGGG!

The phone on his desk scared the hell out of him. The damn thing was too loud.

Cole hurried across the room, placed the gun in the drawer and shut it, and then picked up the receiver. His heart was pounding in his chest.

"Sackler."

"Cole? Is that you?"

Marvin Trent. The boss.

Of course it's me, you ass. I answered the phone by saying, "Sackler!" This happened every single time the guy called.

"Yes, sir."

"Oh, good. It looks like we're all set for tonight, right?"

"As far as I know, sir. The PR firm has handled all the arrangements. No one has sought me out with any problems.

I'm just about to go do a walk-around and make sure everything is on schedule."

"Good, I'm coming to the hotel in about an hour. My wife will join me later, before the start of the event. You have your costume ready for tonight?"

Cole shut his eyes. "I have it, sir."

"Great. I think it's a good idea, don't you? The hotel detective dresses in a mask and costume and mingles with the guests. That way you can hide yourself, keep an eye on *everyone*, and sniff out any trouble before it starts. The guest list is sewn up tightly, but you never know who might be able to sneak in. That serial killer has done it before, you know."

Cole hated the idea of being in disguise for the night. "The security is much better since the renovation, sir. We've hired some good people."

"I know. I designed it myself. But we can't be too careful, right, Cole?"

He cleared his throat. "You're right, sir."

"We can't have anything bad happen tonight. This is the big night. The press will be here, the mayor will be here, New York's beautiful people will be here, and a whole bunch of folks with *money* will be here. We will show the world that Hotel Destiny is ready to serve the best. No more Times Square bottom feeders, if you know what I mean."

"Yes, sir."

"If anyone acts suspicious to you, I expect you to jump on them quickly. The last thing we need is another murder. Jesus. I'd be ruined."

"No, sir. That's not going to happen. Again, I'm sorry I haven't been able to catch the guy who's been—"

"We won't talk about that now, Cole. Let's just get through this evening, and we'll be talking about the future and your role in it in the coming weeks. Okay?"

That didn't sound too promising.

"Okay. Yes, sir."

"Great. See you soon."

The call ended and Cole hung up the phone. With a sigh, he looked at the antique clock on his desk. It was 2:30 in the afternoon. It wouldn't be long before he'd have to shower, shave, and put on the damn cloak and mask.

RRRRRRRIIIIINGGGG!

The damn phone again. What did Trent forget to tell him? He picked up the receiver. "Yes, sir?"

"How polite of you, Mr. Sackler, calling me 'sir.' I like that."

"Oh. Hello, Sergeant Redenius. How are you?"

"Good. Hey, I want to come by and show you some mug shots. Could be connected to our case from February. Hell, it might be connected to all of 'em. You going to be around today?"

"Today isn't good, Sergeant. Tonight is the big Halloween opening gala. We're getting ready for that."

"Oh, that's right, sorry, I forgot about that. Hell, I'm supposed to attend. Did I RSVP? I can't remember."

"Just show up, I'm sure it'll be fine. You can come dressed as a cop."

"Very funny. All right, I may see you tonight, but if not, I'll catch up with you tomorrow, all right?"

Sure, if I'm still alive.

"That's fine, Sergeant."

"Have a good day, then, Sackler."

They hung up and Cole sighed. He then went back to the mirror and felt the stubble on his chin again. There was only one thing he could do over, say, the next hour, to kill some time.

No, two things.

One, have some more Jack Daniel's.

Two, spin the cylinder and play another round of Russian Roulette.

What fun!

2

Guests were already arriving by the time Cole had cleaned up and donned a tuxedo, black cloak with a hood, and a simple white mask that covered the top half of his face. He figured no one would recognize him, but then—he didn't know anyone anyway.

Already with a buzz-on from the alcohol, he left his office-apartment and walked down the corridor past the head manager's office, which was closed and rarely used these days. Trent was certainly never there. Just beyond that on the opposite side of the hall was a dumbwaiter and an employee stairwell and staircase that ascended to the kitchen on the second floor, and down to the basement. This staircase also connected to the fire escape stairs that went all the way up to the twelfth floor.

Cole came to the space behind the front desk, and greeted Virginia, the young woman who worked at the hotel in several capacities, and Carolyn, the PR firm representative in charge of the gala. Virginia was dressed as a witch and Carolyn was a princess.

"Good eeeevening," he said in his best Alfred Hitchcock imitation. "Let me guess, one of you is naughty, the other is nice."

The ladies laughed. "Oh, Mr. Sackler, you look great," Virginia said. "Very dashing."

"Dashing? Really?"

Carolyn added, "You look like you're right out of a Venetian tableau from the turn of the century. Did you arrive in a horse and carriage?"

"Would that be a better transportation option in this city?" He feigned interest in her guest list. "How is everything going so far?"

"Several guests have already arrived. The musicians just started playing. There is a line of limos and taxis pulling up to the front doors. We'll be busy for the next couple of hours."

Cole noted the hired doormen who would also act as bouncers and security men. They checked tickets as costumed visitors entered the building. "Looks like you've got it all under control. Just don't let in any New York Street Skunk."

Carolyn laughed. "Any what?"

Virginia explained, "That's what Cole calls any unwanted riff raff that wander in."

"That's right," Cole said. "New York Street Skunk really *smell*. I'm going up. Bye, ladies."

"Have fun," Virginia said.

He held up a finger and shook his head. "I'm on duty. Absolutely no fun for me."

With that, he walked across the long, rectangular lobby that had been refurbished to resemble Hotel Destiny's 1917 glitz and glamour with a distinct Art Deco style that over the first decade of the century had begun to replace Art Nouveau as the chic and trendy new look. Today, in 1985, the place might have been a wing in a museum. A bas-relief sculpture spread across the lobby's back wall that depicted satyrs and wood nymphs frolicking in the forest. The rest of the walls consisted of a rosewood paneling that evoked the feeling that the space was someone's study. The comfy chairs were also made mostly of oak but with inlays of ivory. The transformation from what the lobby had looked like a year earlier was simply remarkable. Before, it had been a drab, dirty, and intimidating enclosure that was anything but welcoming.

Cole avoided the two main elevators, the doors of which were now covered in a faux gold material, and instead ascended the curving staircase that began next to the elevators on the right. The Grand Stairs had been refurbished with a marble-like flooring that had replaced the seriously gross carpet that had been there for decades. The steps swept up and around to the second-floor foyer, the outer-ballroom area that resembled the lobby in size and shape. The elevator bank was just to one's left after coming up the stairs. The entrance to the Grand Room—the ballroom—was to the right. Picture windows that faced the street adorned the left side of the foyer. At the far end were the men's and women's restrooms, as well as an Employees Only door that accessed a hallway that led behind-the-scenes and to the kitchen, the stairwell that connected to the fire escape staircase, and the steps to the administrative offices one flight down and the basement another level below that. Oddly, the hotel did not have a dedicated restaurant. The kitchen was used only for banquets and other special occasions. Guests normally had to venture out into the New York streets for meals—but there was plenty of fare in the Times Square area, including a diner right around the corner on Seventh Avenue where most people went for breakfast. The hotel kitchen did provide room service, though, on a limited basis, so a chef had always been kept on the payroll.

Dozens of guests in all manner of costumes mingled all over the foyer. Music wafted out of the ballroom through an open door, and Cole headed that way.

The opulence and spectacle on display in the Grand Room, as it had always been called, took the breath away from even a cynic like Coleman Sackler. The ballroom wasn't the kind of huge space that might be at the Waldorf Astoria, but it was adequate for a medium-sized hotel. The color scheme for the party was black and white with splashes of blood-red. While the room could be set up for a banquet, instead of dining tables there were red tablecloth-covered highboys where guests could stand, converse, and enjoy their cocktails. A large square checkerboard dance floor was lit by a magnificent chandelier that hung overhead, set to a Halloween-appropriate level of "dim." Other fixtures threw splashes of bright spots around the room to highlight areas of interest.

A stage at the far end was occupied by a twelve-piece band, the members of which were dressed in sharp suits of the designated period. The music was early jazz—lively and danceable—with a vocalist crooner who delivered numbers like "At the Darktown Strutter's Ball," "For Me and My Gal," and even "Over There," since World War One was at the forefront of the news when the hotel first opened.

A bar on the left side of the room was adorned with Art Deco table lamps that evoked the beginning of the 1920s. Mounted on the opposite wall were two original and restored ten-foot-tall paintings, one of the hotel's original owner, Laurence Flynn, the other of his wife, Theresa. Cole had known the paintings had been kept in the basement storage area since their removal sometime in the 30s or 40s. Now they looked brand new.

Hired women dressed as "flappers" carrying trays of hors d'oeuvres and complimentary champagne flutes slithered in and out of the crowd of guests, which was growing by the minute. Cole knew enough about history to know that the flapper style was a product of the 1920s, and it was a little too early to be represented here for 1917.

The revelers' costumes, of course, were not relegated to that era. There were Draculas, witches, Ronald Reagans, Richard Nixons, Darth Vaders, princesses, sexy nurses, sexy librarians, zombies, Supermen, and, annoyingly to Cole, many men wearing identical tuxes, black cloaks with hoods, and white masks.

What, had there been a fire sale on his choice of disguise?

Cole sighed and decided to head for the bar. He wasn't supposed to drink on the job, but he was in disguise. What the hell. He was going to need to be inebriated before the night was over.

"What's the best whiskey you got?" he asked one of the bartenders, who wore unconvincing Frankenstein's monster makeup.

"Jack and Bushmills. Also have Johnny Walker Scotch."

Cole ordered a double Bushmills since he'd already been swilling Jack Daniel's in his office. Once the drink was in hand, he wandered through the crowd, nodding at various guests who had gone to the trouble to create imaginative costumes. The women were especially spectacular-looking, and if he hadn't been on the job....

After crossing the dance floor, he ended up on the other side of the Grand Room beneath the two paintings of the Flynns. Laurence Flynn had been a kind of *wunderkind* in his day, a wealthy man in his mid-twenties. He had opened Hotel

Destiny when he was only twenty-nine. The wife, Theresa, was blonde and movie-star gorgeous, and that was evident even from a painting. Cole had learned quite a bit about the hotel's history after having worked there for over a decade. The couple was involved in a big scandal that rocked the town, and it had occurred on a Halloween night just like this one, back in 1917. Apparently, Theresa Flynn had been having an affair with an early silent film star by the name of Bradley Granger. The actor was no Clark Gable or George Clooney of his day, but he was something of a minor celebrity.

"She died right upstairs on the third floor," a woman's voice said in Cole's ear.

He turned to see Louise Trent, his boss' twenty-something-year-old daughter. She was dressed as Little Bo Peep, and she, too, had an alcoholic beverage in one hand as well as the iconic shepherd's staff in the other. Blonde, blue-eyed, and too pretty for her own good, she had a reputation of being a wild girl. Every time Cole had come across her, she had mercilessly flirted with him. He couldn't understand what Louise saw in him, but he also didn't want to encourage her. Cole worked for her father.

"I know where Theresa Flynn was killed," Cole answered. "In the 'master apartment,' Room 302, where hotel owners have lived with their families. How are you, Louise? Having fun?"

"Oh, my God! Cole! Is that really you?"

"It is I."

"I didn't recognize you at first! Well, duh, you're wearing a mask. I thought you'd be here acting like the town constable, making sure no one gets out of line."

"That's exactly what I'm doing. Your father wanted me to be in disguise. It's kind of silly, I think, but, you know, orders are orders."

Louise indicated the paintings again. "What do *you* know about them?"

He shrugged. "Not much, really. Just what everyone else does. She was *schtüping* an actor and for some reason the guy shot and killed her, and then shot himself."

"And then her husband did the same thing?"

Cole nodded. "That was over a decade later. He lost a lot of money in the big crash of '29, and he put a gun to *his* head in, what, 1930? 1931?"

"Something like that. You know, they say the hotel is haunted. The Flynns and Granger pop up in the hallways and guest rooms every now and then."

Cole laughed and shook his head. "Well, *I've* never seen them."

She glanced at the glass in his hand. "I see you're working hard."

"Hush. Don't tell your dad."

"I won't if you dance with me."

"Well...."

"Come on."

"I need to survey the place. I have a job to do."

"Later, then?"

"Louise...."

"I'm going to hold you to it, Cole!" She turned, started to walk away, and then looked back at him. "Toodle-oo. And if you find my sheep, don't molest them."

She went off into the crowd. Cole shook his head and continued circling around the room. He set his empty glass on a highboy when he spotted Marvin Trent, a man in his fifties, and his wife among a group of well-known bigwigs and Mayor Ed Koch. The hotel's boss was dressed in a top hat and tails, but with nothing to disguise his face. Cole figured the guy wanted to be recognized when his picture was published in the society pages. He could see where Louise got her looks—from Trent's wife, who was also without a mask.

Cole avoided them and moved on.

The music from the band picked up in tempo as the leader beckoned more guests to the dance floor. Many heeded the call.

Feeling the effects of the whiskey, he stood for a moment by a highboy and scanned the room. He thought he was wasting his time. Nothing bad was going to happen at such a high-profile event.

He did find it extraordinary, though, how many other men had dressed exactly like him. Black cloak and white mask. Weird. He couldn't tell them apart except perhaps by size.

One guy in a cloak and mask stood across the room and seemed to be looking right at Cole. Unmoving, just standing there.

The man looked somewhat familiar.

Cole's body involuntarily jolted, and then he started toward the figure, but a group of dancers moved in his way, jitterbugging or doing the Charleston or whatever kind of step it was.

"Excuse me, folks!" he shouted to be heard over the music. "Excuse me, coming through!"

"Hey, mister, watch out!" a woman snarled at him, but he shoved through the group and got to the other side of the dance floor.

The man in the cloak and mask was gone.

Cole looked in all directions. Sure, he saw *other* men wearing cloaks and masks, but none of them was the one he'd seen.

Am I seeing things?

An unpleasant tingling had come over him when he'd spotted the masked man. What especially disturbed Cole, though, was that this was the same sensation he got when he was in a Dream State and he thought that Charlie, his "brother," was nearby. Cole couldn't explain it, only that it was a peculiar awareness that Charlie's presence was close. He knew, though, that Charlie didn't really exist, even if in Dream States he did.

Right. Ha ha, that was Charlie. *My brother Charlie's at the party. Cole, you're nuts.*

Perhaps it was time for another drink.

He moved toward the bar, but then he sighted a lovely young woman dressed as a gypsy fortune teller sitting behind a card table that was against the wall near the Flynn paintings. He hadn't noticed her before. A little sign on the table read: FREE PALM READINGS. An empty chair was in front of the table. The woman had dark hair and was probably in her mid-twenties. *Very* attractive.

Cole went over to her. "Hello."

"Hello, there, masked man," she said in a thick Eastern European accent. "Would you like to have your fortune told?" She pronounced the word "would" like "vould."

"You're really playing the part, aren't you?"

"What do you mean?" There was a seductive challenge in her voice as her brown eyes focused on him.

"Your accent. You do it well."

"I am sorry, this is the way I really speak. I am from Poland."

"You are? My apologies. I thought you were just a good actress. I didn't notice you earlier. I'm Coleman Sackler, the hotel detective."

"Ah, the hotel detective! They said you would be here...in disguise."

Cole assumed she'd been hired by the PR firm in charge of the gala. "What's your name?"

"Agnieszka." He reached out a hand and she shook it. "So, you want your fortune told or not?"

Cole figured he didn't have anything better to do. "Sure. Lay it on me." He sat in the chair.

"Give me your hand, please."

He did so and allowed her to place his arm and hand on the table, palm up. She carefully spread his fingers and traced the lines on his palm with a fingernail. It tickled, but Cole didn't flinch.

"Did you know," she began, "did you know you can find the truth of your heritage if you take the time to explore this hotel?"

"What?"

"The hotel is quite haunted. Full of ghosts and lost souls from different eras, different years, from all decades since the hotel opened long ago. These lost souls roam freely."

Cole's inclination was to leap from the chair and walk away, but the woman had an amused intensity about her that suggested there might be a punchline at the end. He decided to play along and hear what she had to say.

"The place *was* pretty creepy before it got renovated," he offered. "More sleazy than creepy, really. But I don't believe in ghosts."

"What about the portals? Have you found the portals in the hotel?"

"Portals?"

"If you access the portals and go through them, you can go to other times in the hotel. Other years."

"*What?*" He wanted to laugh.

"Find the portals and you can time travel. But be careful. They are unpredictable and don't always go to the same time." He tried to pull his hand away from the woman, but she held on to him with a firm grip. "You will have vivid memories when you travel through portals," she continued. "You will think you are someplace from your past, but you are really still in the hotel. In truth, you are in compartments that are inside your head and soul."

That sounded a little too familiar.

Is she talking about my Dream States?

"Agnieszka, I don't know what you're talking about...."

"You are in danger, Mr. Sackler. Beware of a man in a black cloak and white mask."

Now she had gone from the playful to the absurd. Cole laughed. "Are you crazy? Look around you! There are dozens of men here in black cloaks and white masks! I'm wearing the same thing!"

She looked at him intently, paused, and whispered, "We have met before, you know."

Cole wrinkled his brow and smiled with cynicism. "We have?"

A smile played on her lips. "Or maybe I met your twin brother."

This prompted a double-take. "What did you say?"

She continued to examine his palm. "I see you were an orphan."

Cole felt a lurch in his chest.

What the fuck? How the hell did she know that?

"Pardon me?"

"You were an orphan. You were orphaned shortly after your birth. You never knew who your real parents were. Am I right?"

Cole's mouth had suddenly gone very dry. His throat felt like sandpaper when he answered, "Yes."

Agnieszka moved back in her chair a little and cocked her head. "You were separated from your twin in the orphanage."

Holy shit! HOLY SHIT!

"Wait, how do you know this? Who are you?"

She shushed him softly and continued to study his hand. "You know his name."

"His name...his name is Charlie."

The woman had totally disarmed him.

"You dream of Charlie," she continued. "You were babies in the orphanage together...and...he is near."

"That's insane," he managed to say.

Agnieszka shook her head. "It is not. It's right here in your palm. You've always wanted to know if Charlie exists."

"Not really!"

"Your parents...your adoptive parents—they thought you just had an imaginary friend when you were young child. Like many children do."

Okay, this has gone from being an impressive parlor trick to the outrageously bizarre....

He tried pulling his hand away again, but he couldn't do it. "Let me go now. I have to—"

"Charlie is close, and you will soon come face to face with him. In fact, you think you just saw him a few minutes ago."

"You're wrong," he said, nervously. "It's my overactive imagination. I've always had one."

"Mr. Sackler," she said, still staring at his palm, "the shadow of your twin is malevolent."

Cole blinked. "What does *that* mean?"

"I see you also suffered severe burns when you were a child."

How in the ever-loving blazing fuck-all does she know THAT?

He sat there with his mouth open. A chill settled in his spine as an unfamiliar emotion overtook him. It had been a long time since he'd known *fear.*

"You wonder how I know this?" she asked. He slowly nodded. "It is my job. I am a fortune teller."

Cole was genuinely shocked. He couldn't protest. Now fully mesmerized by what she had to say, he allowed her to continue the session.

"Yes, you have burned skin. A leg and part of your body."

"My hip and part of my left side," he answered slowly, astonished by what he was hearing.

She nodded. "Happened when you were a baby. Before the orphanage."

"Yes."

"And to your twin, too."

"Charlie. My God, how do you *know* this?"

With her free hand she held up a finger to get him to be quiet. "I see *this*, too. You tried to kill yourself. Not long ago. Today."

Cole emitted a gasp and a shudder. Tears formed in his eyes. "I…don't…how do…?"

"Hush, Mr. Sackler. It is all right."

"I…it was a game."

"A game with a pistol is not a game. Do not do it again."

He swallowed hard. He couldn't stop the tear that ran down his cheek. "I…I won't."

Agnieszka let go of his hand and he swiftly pulled it away. He nursed it in his lap as he stared at the beautiful young woman.

"That is all," she said.

"What?" He wiped his face with his sleeve. She bowed her head slightly and would not look at him. "That's all you have to say? What the hell kind of fortune was that? I can't have you saying crazy things like that to the guests here tonight."

Agnieszka refused to look at him.

That's it. I'm done here.

"Fine." Cole stood abruptly, nearly knocking over the flimsy card table. "Thank you, Agnieszka, that was…very entertaining. I'm going to get a drink now, and then I think I'll have a word with Carolyn at the PR firm about you. Have a good evening."

With that, he walked away and headed for the bar, a little angry and indeed shaken.

3

Cole ordered another double Bushmills and took it with him as he continued to stroll through the groups of costumed revelers. The party was very crowded now. The band was smoking hot and every inch of the dance floor was covered with moving feet.

Still reeling from the encounter with the woman in the gypsy fortune teller costume, Cole filed it away as more New York Street Skunk. He was determined to find out how the PR firm would let someone like that in, but not tonight. He was already feeling the effects of the booze and didn't particularly want to deal with a confrontation.

Back to the job at hand. Was there a serial killer in the room? Cole doubted it. The perp wouldn't dare show his face—or mask—at a party like this. The press, a cop or two, hired bouncers, and tons of witnesses were present. That had to be an adequate deterrent. Besides, the hotel had been renovated and changed since the lowlifes from Times Square and its environs frequented the joint. The place was no longer a dump.

New York Street Skunk was not allowed.

"So, how many drinks is that, Cole?"

He turned to see Little Bo Peep again, still without any sheep. She did still have her trusty staff and another glass of something.

"I don't know, Louise, how many is that for you?"

"Five!" She raised the glass a little too exuberantly with that announcement and spilled some of the liquid on the floor. She was obviously telling the truth.

"Slow down, Louise. It's still early. You should pace yourself. At the rate you're going, you won't make it to ten o'clock."

"Shut up, Cole. You're supposed to dance with me. Come on, you ready now?"

"Oh, geez, Louise, really? Look how crowded it is over there."

"It's more fun that way. You can meet people."

"I don't care to meet people."

"Come on, don't be a wallflower. Did you really just say 'geez, Louise'?" She rested her staff against a nearby highboy and placed her drink on top. She then reached over and took his glass and did the same with it. Cole let her grab his hand and lead him to a corner of the checkerboard square as the band launched into a rousing version of "Has Anybody Seen My Gal?" Cole put his arm around her waist, grasped her right hand with his left, and then they went at it.

Cole hadn't realized just how drunk Louise was until she started dancing. He had no excuses for himself, but what was hers? Was she unhappy? She came from a very wealthy family and probably would never have to work a day in her life. He'd occasionally seen her at the hotel during the renovations and gotten to know her slightly. She had always seemed fine then, but at those times she didn't have a drink in her hand. Maybe she was just an easy drunk and liked to party.

"Have you had your fortune told yet?" he shouted at her as they moved clumsily, sometimes bumping into other dancers.

"What do you mean?"

"There's a fortune teller over there—" Cole gestured to the wall where the Flynn portraits hung, but Agnieszka and her table were gone. He scanned the area and didn't see her. "Well, she was over there. She was dressed like a gypsy. I guess Carolyn or someone shooed her away. She was very odd."

"I didn't see her. Was she an old lady?"

"No. Young. About your age. Quite attractive, I guess." He wrinkled his brow, wondering what the heck really could have happened to Agnieszka.

Louise reached up and pinched his mouth, puckering it up. "Don't worry about her, handsome. Little Bo Peep doesn't have any sheep tonight, so she'll be a lot more fun than some old gypsy lady."

Handsome?

Cole looked at her and Louise wiggled her eyebrows, as if attempting to communicate something to him.

Was she coming on to him?

He kept hold of her as the band segued into "Moonlight Bay." Louise started laughing hysterically as Cole managed to keep her moving. He thought all the flirtation was a result of the booze, but what the hell…he welcomed the attention.

"What's so funny?" he shouted.

"You! Me! All of us! I'm having a ball, aren't you?"

Not particularly, but I want to know if the foreplay that's going on is serious.

They continued to dance, spin, and watch the sea of characters around them.

Then Cole saw him.

The man in the black cloak and white mask. The same one as before. He stood against the wall beneath the Flynn paintings, almost on the same spot where Agnieszka's table had been.

The man was staring at them.

"Do you know that guy over there?" Cole asked.

Louise turned her head. "Who?"

"See the guy with the cloak and white mask? He's standing just under the paintings. See?"

She did one of those laughs that were accompanied by a raspberry noise. "You kidder! How could I recognize him if he's wearing a mask?"

"But do you see him?"

"I see him."

"You've never seen him before?"

"How would I know, dummy? He's wearing a fucking mask!"

"Oh, never mind."

The dance kept going, although both were exhibiting signs of pooping out.

"You know," she said loudly into his ear, "it's a real drag being the daughter of society-darling parents. Sometimes I wish I was just a normal middle-class girl."

He chuckled and told her, "I'd be happy to turn you into one."

"Yeah? Well, let's go to your office for a little bit and seal the deal."

That threw him. "What?"

"Come on. You're single now, right? Your divorce was, what, three years ago?"

"Louise. It's not a good idea. I work for—"

"—my father, I know. Screw him. On second thought, I'd rather screw you. What do you say? Before we all turn into pumpkins here."

Cole wondered if she really knew what she was doing. He didn't want to take advantage of someone who was...but that thought got interrupted and made a left turn. Marvin Trent was possibly going to fire him soon. Everything had been leading up to it. The boss wanted to get through the grand opening, and then the axe was going to fall. Cole knew it. It was inevitable. He was a drunk and a grouch and bad at his job. So...why the hell should he not accept a blatant invitation from Trent's daughter?

He led her off the dance floor.

"Wait, wait," she said.

"What?"

"I have to go to the ladies' room. Powder my nose. You know. Can I meet you in your office?"

He looked at her. "Are you sure about this, Louise? You're not too...uh, plastered?"

"Not at all. Go on to your office. That way no one will see us together. I'll be there in fifteen minutes." She walked away, a little unsteadily, but she seemed to be handling herself all right.

Cole glanced back at the wall where the paintings hung. The cloaked, masked man was no longer standing there.

Charlie, are you here, brother?

He shook himself like a dog, as if ridding himself of the nagging discomfort he'd been feeling after having his "fortune" told and seeing the man in the mask. He grabbed his drink from the highboy and brought it with him as he quickly moved across the ballroom toward the doors. He'd had enough playing hotel detective for the night. A dalliance with the boss' daughter was far more appealing.

Once he was in the outer foyer, there was a hop to his steps. He descended the stairs two at a time to the lobby.

"Has anybody seen my gal...?" he softly sang to himself.

The anticipation of what was about to happen behind closed doors was delicious.

He nodded at Virginia, who was alone behind the reception desk. "How's it going?"

"Just fine, Cole."

"You might see Louise Trent come through here in a bit. It's something related to the hotel."

"Okay."

He lifted the section of counter, swung open the waist-high door, and practically skipped into the hallway that led to his office and apartment.

Once inside, he left the door open, took a final swig from his whiskey, and set the empty glass on his desk.

Too bad the place is so dingy. Oh well, a bed is a bed is a bed....

Cole quickly sailed into the bedroom, picked up some discarded clothing, and threw them in the clothes hamper in his closet. He did a cursory straightening of the bedsheets, and then went back into the office. He then stood in front of the mirror and removed his mask. The eyes were still a little bloodshot, but he didn't appear too worse for wear. As a token to kinkiness, he replaced the mask on his face and grinned in the mirror.

"Has any-bod-y seen my gal?" he sang again as he straightened his bow tie.

There was movement behind him in the reflection.

Someone had entered the office.

Ah, she's here already!

Still looking in the mirror, Cole watched the figure emerge from the shadows. He expected Little Bo Peep, but instead it was the man in the cloak and white mask.

Cole reflexively started to turn, but the man's approach was fast and catlike. A raised pistol pointed at his head, and it fired without warning.

There was no time for a scream.

The final image that Cole registered as he began to topple was the sudden splatter of blood and bits of skull and brains on the mirror.

And then nothingness.

4

There was the sound of strong winds, as if a hurricane or tornado were raging.

Confusion. Disorientation. Blackness.

And yet...Cole was *aware* of all these things. He had a consciousness.

He didn't feel the wind. He only heard it.

His mind told an arm to reach out, but he wasn't sure if the command was heeded. He wasn't entirely positive that he *had* an arm. Nevertheless, upon thinking that he'd completed the action, the wind subsided a little. Cole couldn't see anything, though. Not his arm or hand, not a space in front of him...only darkness. A void without light.

And he was floating in it. Or his mind was. Something.

Very puzzling.

It was also odd that he wasn't panicking. He might have been terribly baffled, but he was also calm.

Was he asleep? That's it, he was dreaming! He was in some new form of Dream State, something he hadn't experienced before.

No...wait.

He'd been shot.

That he remembered.

It all started to come back to him.

He'd been in his office at Hotel Destiny, looking in the mirror, waiting for...what's-her-name. Little Bo Peep. *Louise.* That's it. Louise Trent.

Yes, that final scene was forming as a picture in his mind.

There was also a hazy illumination in front of him now. The more he remembered, the brighter it became.

The man in the cloak and mask. A gun.

Oh, Christ, I was shot! Am I in a coma? Am I dead?

He reached out again with a hand—and there was vague movement in the shadows in front of him.

Yes, that was his arm and hand.

A sensation of *standing* returned to him. His feet were firmly planted on a hard surface. Could he take a step? He willed it so...and sure enough, he felt a body—*his* body—move forward. As he did so, his surroundings became a little less dark. Now there was a dimness in front of him, and he could make out that he was standing in a corridor of some kind. Very narrow. Room enough for only one person. Black walls—or curtains? Only the immediate few feet of the corridor were visible in a now-shimmering light that barely revealed its presence. Beyond that was more darkness, stretching to a one-point perspective of black emptiness.

He stepped forward and again the lighting brightened slightly. More of the hallway revealed itself. It was as if someone behind-the-scenes was slowly pushing up a dimmer whenever he moved. He was also now aware that he was wearing dark clothing, but he couldn't tell what it was. At least he wasn't naked.

Cole attempted to speak.

Hello?

He didn't hear himself. The wind sound, though, had died down to almost nothing. It had been replaced by a ticking. Like a clock. In seconds.

Tick-tick-tick-tick-tick-tick-tick-tick....

Where the fuck am I? What the hell is going on?

Stepping forward apparently made the light grow brighter, so he did so again. Now he could see shapes on the two walls that stretched into the distance. Frames.

Paintings?

No, photographs. Maybe.

Cole took several steps and was eventually in front of one on the wall to his left.

Oh, my God!

It was an image of his adoptive parents. Fred and Florence Sackler. She was holding a baby and he was looking on with pride.

Cole had seen that photograph in his home when he was growing up. That baby was *him*! The picture had been taken not long after the Sacklers had adopted him from the orphanage.

A few feet ahead, on the right side of the wall was another framed photograph. He moved forward to see that it revealed a small boy, maybe three or four years old, sitting beside a Christmas tree. He looked happy and surprised as he held up a toy fire truck.

That was him, too. Cole remembered the photo being in a family album.

A few more steps and there was another frame on the left. This one featured a picture of young Cole, maybe five or six, at his own birthday party. Three or four other boys were with him. He recalled that they were faces of playmates, but the friendships didn't last. Their names were lost to him. Cole never had a "best friend" when he was a child.

Why not? he wondered, maybe for the first time.

He didn't know this photograph. Cole was pretty sure he'd never seen it before.

Moving on, there was yet another framed photo on the right. Again, he didn't know this image ever existed in physical form. He remembered the incident, though. Cole was seven and his mother had just dropped him off at school to begin first grade. He'd started crying. Other children had made fun of him. His mother was embarrassed. The teacher wasn't supportive. She had told him to shut up and be a big boy, that he was in first grade now!

That day had been very traumatic.

Cole moved on and then there he was at eight years old. Bullies at his school were picking on him. They performed that old dirty trick on Cole. One boy sneaked behind Cole and got on his hands and knees, and then the other kid, facing Cole, pushed him. Cole fell backwards over the henchman. Laughter. Humiliation.

No one had photographed the incident. How was it that the scene was displayed here?

Then he got it. He'd always heard that your life flashes before your eyes when you die. Was that what was happening here? Did it mean he was dead? The corridor displayed moments of Cole's life. Memories. He imagined that if he kept moving forward, he would glimpse pieces of everything he had ever done.

Cole wasn't sure he wanted to do that.

He turned around, attempting to go back the other direction, but he couldn't see the distance he had already traveled. It was just a wall of shadow. Cole attempted to move into it—but couldn't! The darkness was like an invisible wall. It prevented him from going backwards.

There was only one direction to go—forward down the corridor.

Fine. He simply wouldn't look at the framed photographs. They disturbed him.

Cole walked at a faster pace, barely glancing at the images on either side of him.

What had happened to him? Why did the man in the cloak and mask shoot him? Cole reached up and felt his head—and he *could!* He touched hair. A forehead, eyes, a nose, a mouth, a chin. Everything was intact. It was all there. No gunshot wound.

Was the man in the mask the mad serial killer who had left several bodies in the hotel? Why did Louise want him to go to his office and meet her there? Had she set him up? Cole recalled spotting the masked man at the party. The guy had been closely watching Cole. Had he come to the event expressly to murder Cole? And if so, *why?*

Was the man...*Charlie?*

Was his twin brother the serial killer?

The shadow of your twin is malevolent.

Someone had said that to him recently. A woman. Who was it? Not Louise. He couldn't recall.

Eventually, Cole came to a draped archway on the left. Dark, black curtains were pulled back to reveal an opening. He stopped in front of the space. Should he go that way? It wasn't very welcoming. However, the corridor with the picture frames seemed to go on and on into infinity. It made sense to see where this intersection led him.

Cole stepped out of the corridor, through the archway, and found himself in a dark room that had a completely different ambiance. There was no more wind noise. The ticking had stopped.

He felt his body was more intact.

In front of him was a door. He could *see* it. A sliver of light was at the bottom, indicating that beyond the door was real brightness.

He thrust out a hand like a blind man and touched a solid, wood door. There was a knob. He turned it, and the door opened outward.

Cole stepped out of a clothes closet and into a room identical to his office-bedroom at Hotel Destiny.

What the hell?

He turned around and found that he was standing in a small clothes closet with a wall in the back. No archway, no drapes. How did he get here?

The closet was empty. In fact, the bedroom, too, was vacant, save for an old-fashioned sofa, coffee table, and a couple of chairs. The furniture looked brand new, but they weren't modern. He was certain it was his bedroom at the hotel, though. The one window was the same, and the view, like the one in his office, revealed the back of a brick building that stood behind the hotel.

Cole closed the closet door and then moved across the room to face another door, the one that would go to his office. He put an ear to it, listened, and heard silence. He turned the knob and pushed the door open.

Yes. His office. And it looked pretty much the way he'd left it. The same decades-old desk and furniture.

But the desk looked clean and new and fresh and slick.

The Parisian rug wasn't faded anymore. The blue and gray colors were vibrant, and all the swirly paisley shapes were discernible, unlike the way they were when he usually occupied the office.

Lighting came from a lamp on the desk that he hadn't had before, and from another standing lamp near the mirror, which was still on the wall. The glass was clean, polished, and shiny.

Cole stepped over and looked at his reflection.

He was still wearing the damned black cloak and white mask.

Ripping off the mask revealed a face he recognized as himself. Clean, shaven, with slightly bloodshot eyes. No gunshot wound.

Well, let's see what's outside.

He opened the office door and stepped into the hallway. He heard faint music in the distance. Cole carefully walked to the reception desk. No one was there. A couple of men, also dressed in cloaks and masks, manned the front doors of the hotel and welcomed costumed guests coming in from the street.

There was a big party in progress, but it wasn't the one at which he'd been before.

Cole crossed the lobby, which appeared pristine and new, but not the remodeled "new" as it had been when he'd last seen it. He made for the curving staircase and ascended it. Oddly, much of the electrical lighting was not present in the lobby or on the stairs. Instead, candelabras provided most of the illumination.

On the second floor, guests milled around outside the Grand Room as before. Big band music wafted in from the ballroom.

Cole replaced the mask on his face.

He stepped into the Grand Room and gasped.

The big chandelier was present and dimly lit, but many more Art Deco lamps populated the big room. The bar was still on the left. The portraits of Laurence and Theresa Flynn adorned the right wall. A big band occupied the stage and were playing the same songs he'd heard at the Halloween party, but the band members were different.

And the people! Yes, they were in costumes, but something was very different. The way they moved. Their demeanors. They seemed more...refined?

The costumes also seemed to be of another era. Many men work black cloaks and white masks, more so than before. Women were dressed more elegantly and carried masks on sticks that they would occasionally hold to their faces. There were no Draculas, Supermen, Darth Vaders, sexy librarians, sexy nurses, or any pop culture figures.

The kicker was the banner that spread from left to right above the stage. It read: HOTEL DESTINY GRAND OPENING— HALLOWEEN 1917.

5

Cole immediately reversed direction and returned to the ballroom outer foyer. He backed against a wall and attempted to control his breathing. His heart pounded in his chest and he felt as if he couldn't get enough air in his lungs. He was hyperventilating.

Where before he had been relatively calm, *now* he was in panic mode.

What kind of trick had been played on him? Was it an elaborate hoax?

Guests walked past him but didn't look at him. It was as if he wasn't there.

Cole needed a drink. That would help. The surge of sweet, lovely alcohol coursing through his bloodstream would do the trick.

He took a deep breath, attempted to settle himself, and then walked back into the ballroom. He headed straight to the bar, held up a finger, and called, "Bartender!"

The man behind the counter ignored him.

"Hey, you, bartender!"

Nothing.

There was a tray of recently filled flutes of champagne waiting to be picked up by one of the male servants working the party. No flappers—or women—serving drinks here. Cole simply took a glass and downed it. The bubbly liquid was a heaven-sent nectar that immediately ignited his senses. He slammed the empty glass back on the tray and took another. Again, the sparkling burn was a welcome sensation in his throat and all the way down his esophagus. It was good stuff, too. Much better than the cheaper swill that had been served at the other party.

Cole looked around him. He couldn't really be standing in the year 1917...could he?

Impossible. It was a ruse. Marvin Trent had probably arranged it. He wanted to freak out the night manager/hotel detective before firing him.

Cole finished the second glass and picked up a third. That one he nursed slowly and began to walk around the room. A couple almost bumped into him; he moved to the side and said, "Excuse me," but they didn't acknowledge him. "I said *excuse me!*" he snarled back at them, but they kept walking toward the bar.

An attractive woman stood watching the couples on the dance floor. She held a glass of champagne and she swayed a little to the music. Cole approached her.

"Are you alone?" he asked.

She didn't look at him.

"Hello?"

Nothing.

He waved a hand in front of her face and she didn't register it.

No. This can't be happening.

Cole moved on and attempted to talk to a group of men who were discussing the stock market. "Hi gents. If this is really 1917, then get your shit out of the market before 1929. That's the best advice I can give you!"

No one paid any attention to him.

They can't hear me. They can't see me. I'm invisible to them all.

And yet he could pick up a glass of champagne and drink it. Could they see *that?*

Cole held out his glass in front of one man's face. He didn't register it. Cole then poured the rest of the contents on the man's jacket. *That* he noticed!

"What in the world?" he gasped with a jump. He looked up, thinking the spill had come from the ceiling. He brushed the liquid off and then asked his friends, "Did you see that? Where the hell did this come from?"

His buddies were looking around, too.

"Which one of you did this? Brand new tuxedo, too!"

They all proclaimed their innocence in the matter, but the man went off in a huff toward the foyer and the men's room.

Cole thought about what had just occurred. So...apparently, he was invisible. He could touch and manipulate objects in the world around him, but as soon as they were in his possession, they became invisible, too. The champagne was no longer on his person when he poured it out of the glass; hence his victim could see and feel the liquid as it splashed onto his jacket.

Very weird.

I need to get out of here. Leave the hotel.

He threw his empty glass against the wall, where it shattered. Several people turned to see what had caused the noise and then looked around them for the culprit. "Who did that?" one woman asked.

Cole strode to the door, went through the foyer, and ran down the stairs to the lobby. He aimed straight for the front of the building, swept past a doorman, and pushed open a door that normally opened to the street around the corner from Seventh Avenue.

He was met with a tremendous black wall of wind. The noise was excruciating, the visibility was blinding, and he was unable to step into the maelstrom. Cole screamed, retreated, and pulled the door closed.

"God!" he coughed. He took several deep breaths. "What the hell was that?"

And yet...and yet when he peered out the glass in the door, the street appeared to be clear of any kind of weather. The moon shone brightly, and a horse and carriage stood in front, its coachman helping an elegantly dressed lady out of her seat. An old-fashioned automobile, a Ford Model T vintage—Cole didn't know his history of cars—honked and drove around the carriage.

Cole shoved open the door again—and the dark hurricane barrier struck him harder. He attempted to push himself into the chaos, but the force and power of the obstacle was too much. Giving up, he pulled the door shut and fell back onto the lobby floor.

"Why does this door keep opening?" a doorman asked

someone who had appeared next to him.

"Maybe the latch is broken?"

"No, there, it's closed now. Huh. Must be a flaw. I'll have to speak to Mr. Flynn about it so he can point it out to the architect."

"Do you fellas not see me?" Cole asked.

They didn't. The men went about their business, greeting guests and giving directions.

Cole stood, brushed himself off…and then he wanted to scream. He couldn't leave the hotel. Something was keeping him there for a reason, and he was determined to find out what it was.

He dejectedly ascended the stairs again. Maybe there would be some answers in the ballroom. For a moment he was alone before stepping foot on the second floor. He felt tears forming in his eyes. He didn't think he could deal with this. None of it. It wasn't fair. What kind of life was he going to have, stuck in the goddamned hotel and no one able to see or hear him?

Cole entered the ballroom and shouted, "Why can't anyone see me?"

Everyone nearby turned and looked at him, startled by his outburst. A few of them laughed. "We see you, mister," some woman said. "Go get a drink, buster," a man prompted, not too kindly.

He stood there with his mouth open. *What?*

The crowd turned back to their conversations. A server offered him a glass of champagne from a tray. "No, thanks," he said. "I need something stronger."

He went to the bar, where the bartender was smiling and watching him. The man had heard Cole's eruption at the door.

"Take it easy, buddy," he said. "Have a drink. What can I get you?"

"Whiskey. Whatever you have."

"Coming up."

Cole was very confused now. The bartender had heard him. People could see him.

What the hell was going on?

The bartender slid the full glass to him. "Here you are, sir."

"You can see me?" Cole asked him.

The bartender winked at him. "Do you want to be seen?"

"Yes!"

"Then I can see you. Relax. Have a good time." The man left him and went to attend to other guests.

Cole chugged a third of the whiskey, letting the harsh but welcome burn coat his insides. He then remained at the bar and continued to sip the drink. Slowly, he began to feel less anxious.

Was he in a Dream State? No, that couldn't be the case. In his Dream States, Cole would remember his own past and relive events. This was something totally new. It wasn't a sleeping dream, because he'd already pinched himself a couple of times. No, he was awake. This was all real.

After he finished the whiskey, Cole set about wandering around the room again. In one corner, a group of men in top hats were smoking cigars, talking, and laughing. Some of them wore masks, but one man didn't—and Cole recognized him. He was Laurence Flynn, owner of Hotel Destiny. The painting on the wall didn't do him justice. Flynn looked a little older than his twenty-nine years, and he appeared to be in good spirits. He looked over at Cole and smiled.

"Hello there, sir, welcome to the party." Flynn held out his hand. "I'm Laurence Flynn." Cole hesitantly shook his hand. He was dazed and quite out of it. "And you are...?"

"Oh, sorry. Coleman Sackler. Very...nice to meet you."

"And you as well. I hope you're having a good time."

"Yes. Thank you."

"Do you work in the financial district?"

"Huh?"

"I'm sorry. From whom did you receive the invitation to the party?"

"I...don't know."

Flynn perceived that he wasn't getting anywhere with this particular guest who probably already had had too much to drink—so he nodded politely, said, "Well, have a good evening, sir," and then turned back to his friends to continue their conversation.

Cole ambled away from them and found himself near the wall that boasted the two portraits of the Flynns.

There, at a card table, was Agnieszka, still dressed as a gypsy fortune teller. The little sign on the table read: FREE PALM READINGS.

Her eyes were on him, and a smile played around her mouth.

Wait.

Cole shut his eyes and looked at her again.

It was impossible. The pretty woman looked exactly the way she did in 1985. Now he *knew* this was one big sick joke, a trick that had been played on him. Everyone in the ballroom was in on it.

He went up to her.

"Oh, it's you," she said, batting her eyelids with intentional flirtation. "Back for more?"

"What is happening to me?"

She gazed at him with amusement. After a beat, she said, "Sit down, and I will tell you."

6

Cole reluctantly sat across from Agnieszka. He was immediately entranced by her brown eyes, which seemed to look past his skin and into the depths of his consciousness. He found her to be confounding, to be sure, and yet equally bewitching. Cole briefly thought that in a completely different situation, he might have fallen in love with this woman.

"Well?" he asked.

"Ask me the question that is on your mind."

"Am I dead?"

She studied him for a moment and then gently answered, "Yes, you are."

Cole felt a stab of sorrow in his chest, for he knew she spoke the truth. He had been in denial ever since he'd "awoken" from being murdered. Although he didn't understand what was happening to him *now*, Cole accepted that this was indeed his fate.

"I am, too, by the way," Agnieszka said. "Have you noticed that no one here can see me either?"

Cole looked around at all the party revelers. None of them looked their way.

"You're right. Why is it that they usually don't see or hear me, but then sometimes they can?"

"Because you *can* appear to the living when you want to. There's a…trick to it. You have to learn how to do it."

"And how do I do that?"

"You have seen movies and read books about ghosts, am I right? Throughout history, people have spoken about 'seeing a ghost' and sometimes even talking to one. One minute the ghost is there, and then it is gone. You can do that. It takes practice, but once you figure out the method, you will be able to do it. You will find that you can appear to living people and interact with them, touch them, and they can do the same to you. You will feel things, just as you did when you were alive. You have already seen that you can drink and feel the effects of alcohol. Your human senses have not changed."

"I don't know if that will be good or bad."

"Oh, you will feel pain, if that is your concern. The good thing is that people cannot physically harm you. Have no fear in that regard. Any damage your body takes while you're 'visible' will quickly disappear. You can't die *twice*."

"You sound like you know the ropes," Cole said. "What happened to you? Who are you really?"

"I told you that my name is Agnieszka. I am from Poland. I worked in this country as a maid. In fact, I worked in this hotel as a maid. I died in this hotel. Look, this is how I *really* appear."

With that, a shadow passed over her face, and Agnieszka was suddenly covered in blood. A quarter of her skull and black hair was blown away, the muscle and tissue and brains loosely hanging out. It was a most horrific sight, causing Cole to shout with repulsion. He lifted an arm to cover his eyes.

"Come, come, Mr. Sackler," she said. "It's not as bad as that."

He peered over the top of his limb and saw that her face was back to normal. Hesitantly, he lowered his arm. "Please don't do that again."

She chuckled softly and shook her head. "That's what someone looks like who has been shot in the head by a gun. It's not pretty."

"Wait. Are you—?"

Agnieszka cocked her head at him.

"Are you the maid who was killed in the boiler room in the hotel? In 1972?"

An expression of sadness streamed over her face, and Cole knew that the answer to his question was affirmative.

"Who did it?" he asked.

She didn't answer him. Instead, Agnieszka said, "A lost soul—a ghost—sometimes has a task to complete that wasn't fulfilled while he or she was alive. It depends on the case, but often if we solve a problem that was there when we were alive, then our cursed existence in this netherworld will end."

"I was murdered by a man wearing a black cloak and a white mask," Cole said.

"Then perhaps you need to find out who he was. Maybe that will provide peace to your soul."

"Really?"

"I told you before that this hotel holds the key to your heritage. In order to solve your murder, you must find out the truth about yourself. The answers lie within Hotel Destiny. An apt name, yes?"

"Is this why I can't leave the building?"

She nodded. "That is correct. On the other hand, you may prefer to stay. Many do."

The conversation wasn't making Cole feel very confident. He may have been the hotel detective, but he wasn't particularly good at solving crimes, as revealed by the serial killings that had occurred during his employment.

"What is it that *you* need to solve?" he asked.

"That is my business," she answered firmly. "Besides, sometimes the thing you need to fix cannot be mended. Perhaps heaven—or hell—is wandering the hotel as a lost soul for eternity."

"I can't see how that would be heaven."

"Why not? I told you of the portals. You find them, and then you can visit other years in which the hotel existed. Mind you, these years will be only significant ones that have to do with your legacy."

"What do you mean? My heritage, my legacy…stop talking in riddles."

"Perhaps 'birthright' is a better word."

"Are you talking about the fact that I was an orphan?"

She made a face that said, *maybe yes, maybe no.*

"This is 1917, isn't it?" he asked.

"Yes."

"What could this year possibly have to do with my 'heritage,' as you call it?"

"That is for you to find out."

"You're full of riddles and puzzles, but no answers, Agnieszka. It's starting to annoy me."

"I help you how I can."

He impatiently looked around the room. The party was still going on, although it felt as if he'd been forever sitting in that chair across from the "gypsy."

"So, how do I find the portals? Where are they?"

"I don't know."

"What do you mean, you don't know?"

"Usually you find one by accident. And, as I said before, you will find that you will relive moments of your life, or, more often, be an observer of moments from your life. Have you noticed anything unusual about time?"

"Time? You mean minutes, hours? I haven't been here that long to notice anything."

"Time will play games with you, no matter where you are or *when* you are. It can sometimes be like an edit in a film. It might be one o'clock in a room you're standing in. You look out a window for what you think is a few seconds, but when you turn back to the clock on the wall it says four. Or a day later. Or a year. It is unpredictable, I'm afraid."

"Great. I think I need another drink."

She smiled at him. "Has anyone ever told you that you drink too much, Mr. Sackler?"

"Plenty of times."

She shrugged. "Go get your drink."

Cole stood. "Thanks for the...tips?" He shook his head. "This is fucking nuts." He turned and walked toward the bar.

The bartender acknowledged him. "Same as before, sir?"

"Yeah, double whiskey."

The man poured it and slid the glass over. Cole thanked him, picked up the drink, and turned to head back to Agnieszka.

Both she and her table were gone.

7

Grumbling to himself, Cole scanned the Grand Room with his eyes to see if Agnieszka may have merely moved her table, but of course she hadn't, she had simply vanished. After all, she had admitted to being a ghost. Cole, however, still wasn't totally convinced that *he* was also one. Never mind that people in the ballroom could see him and talk to him one minute, and then the next minute they couldn't.

He went out to the foyer to see if she might be there, but for once the space was empty. Everyone was inside the ballroom or in the bathrooms or downstairs in the lobby. The Grand Stairs, which curved from the lobby to the second-floor foyer, had another extension that ascended to the third floor, where most of the VIP "suites" were located. During his tenure at the hotel, the suites had been trashed and unusable, but in the building's heyday they were the most elegant rooms in the hotel. In fact, he knew that the Flynn family had lived in the largest suite, called the Apartment, which contained three bedrooms along with a private kitchen, dining room, and living room.

What in the world had Agnieszka meant by his "heritage"? What was he supposed to find in the year 1917 that had anything to do with his own life? Still anxious, angry, and not just a little frightened, Cole figured that he should perhaps attempt to solve the puzzle. What did he have to lose? He was a hotel detective, damn it! He could *do* this!

Before he could begin his investigation, though, Cole found he needed to use the men's room—*How come a ghost has to pee? Weird!*—so he went into the gents'. A man in his thirties, impeccably dressed as one of the Three Musketeers, was washing his hands at one of the basins. He had a fake mustache and beard that he had removed for a moment.

"Some party, eh?" Cole said to him, but the man didn't register being addressed. "Hello? Hey, Douglas Fairbanks, or whoever you are, I'm talking to you."

Nothing. Cole was invisible again. How did that happen?

The man at the sink looked in the mirror and reapplied the mustache and beard, and then spoke drunkenly to his reflection. "You are the most handsome fella here! Go get her!" With a hiccup, the man turned and for a second had a little trouble controlling his equilibrium. He finally made his way out of the bathroom.

Cole did his business at a urinal, washed his hands—*Do ghosts carry germs? Habits are habits!*—and then left the bathroom. He saw the musketeer standing and speaking quietly with an absolutely gorgeous blonde woman. After a double-take, Cole recognized her. Theresa Flynn, wife of the hotel owner and manager. Her painting hung on the wall in the ballroom. She was dressed in an extravagant corset and large French court dress from Marie Antoinette's era—in fact, that was who she was for Halloween, for she had painted a red, bloody line around her neck.

The couple was whispering conspiratorially. She placed a hand on the side of his face, looked around to make sure no one was watching, and then kissed his cheek. The man attempted to *really* kiss her, but she stopped him, whispered something else, and then pushed him away. The musketeer turned and ascended the stairs toward the third floor. Theresa Flynn then held her head high and returned to the ballroom.

They hadn't seen Cole at all. He was invisible.

Theresa Flynn appeared to be having a clandestine rendezvous with a man who wasn't her husband! Then Cole remembered—at the time of her death, she was allegedly having an affair with silent film star Bradley Granger. Was that Granger? The man was quite intoxicated. Had he gone up to his room? If it was on the third floor, then he would be wealthy enough to afford a suite. Yes, that very well could have been him.

Was *this* the fateful night for those two? Of course it was!

The murder/suicide occurred on the night of Hotel Destiny's gala opening.

Cole went back into the ballroom and looked for Theresa Flynn. Perhaps he could stop her from going upstairs later and meeting her doom. The first thing he needed to do, though, was figure out the trick Agnieszka told him about that allows him to be seen and heard by the living. So far, there had been no rhyme or reason as to how it was done.

He concentrated. *Be seen! Be seen!*

A server walked past him. "Excuse me," he said, but the man ignored him.

He moved to the bar and attempted to attract the bartender's attention, but it was no use. Cole then strained his body, clenched his fists, shut his eyes tightly, and grunted. After a few seconds, he relaxed and then called to the bartender. Still no good.

Damn it.

The bartender set a tray of filled champagne flutes on the bar as a server reached for it. Cole quickly scooped up a glass just before the man took it away. He drank it down, placed the empty glass on the bar, and then walked away.

Unlike at the 1985 party, here there were groups of comfy chairs and coffee tables where guests could sit, smoke, drink, and talk if they didn't want to dance. Cole passed one group in the corner where a few men were smoking and holding glasses of champagne. They were surrounded by young women, as if they were celebrities. Cole moved closer and saw that the men were indeed famous. He recognized two of them, anyway. None other than Mary Pickford and Harry Houdini were conversing and laughing at something. The older gentleman near them seemed to be bemused by the two, but had a more erudite demeanor about him, as if he were superior to the filmmaker/actor and the illusionist.

"Mr. Edison," Pickford said, "I hope you will come to California soon and pay us a visit. Southern California is always beautiful."

"I don't particularly like Hollywood, Miss Pickford," the man said. "As you know, most of those other studio upstarts took me to court a few years ago."

Holy cow, Cole thought, *that's Thomas Edison!* The guy who invented the phonograph and the light bulb and motion picture cameras and stuff.

If he'd been visible, Cole might have said hello to the VIPs, but since he wasn't….

He moved on to another seating area where several attractive young women were conversing. He heard the name "Theresa" mentioned, so Cole decided to stand near them and eavesdrop.

"She's a wonderful hostess," a tall bird-like woman dressed as a witch said. "She will be a regular feature in the society pages, don't you think?"

There were affirmative answers, but one lady who was costumed as a princess spoke softly. "Of course she will, but you know she is not beyond providing extra services for certain personages to gain favors."

"Dorothy!" the witch gasped. "What a terrible thing to say!"

Another woman, who was disguised as a bride, said, "It's true, Violet. If you ask me, Theresa is just using Laurence's money and status to advance herself in society."

Dorothy nodded, "I heard that Laurence wants more children, but she doesn't."

Violet asked, "How old is little Miranda?"

"Three."

"Well, she should have brothers and sisters. It's a wife's duty."

Dorothy leaned in and whispered, "Do you know what I've heard about Theresa and that movie star?"

Violet cleared her throat loudly, and said, "Theresa! *Lovely* party, my dear!"

Theresa Flynn had approached them but had not heard their gossip. "Are you enjoying yourselves, ladies?"

"Absolutely!"

"The hotel is beautiful!"

"Thank you," Theresa said. "I had a little say on how the ballroom should look. Laurence is very happy with the place." She gathered her huge dress and sat for a moment on the edge of a sofa. "Did you see Mary Pickford? She's here talking to Harry Houdini!"

"We did! I was thrilled to see her. And him, too!"

"Is there anyone else famous here?" Violet asked.

"There is, but I can't think of them all, my head is all fluttery. Bradley Granger was here earlier, but he left. Oh, Thomas Edison is here! Fanny Brice was supposed to come but she was a no-show."

"Oh, that's too bad."

"Well, enjoy yourselves, I must mingle." Theresa stood, straightened the over-the-top dress, and waved goodbye.

When the hostess was out of earshot, Dorothy said, "So, Bradley Granger *was* here. Hm."

Cole had had enough. He moved on and once again concentrated on being seen.

Hey, look at me! I can be seen! I can be seen!

Nothing happened. It was no use. He'd never figure it out.

The band struck up another set after an apparent break, and many of the guests swarmed to the dance floor. Cole meandered back to where Laurence Flynn was talking with other men. The subject was still money and investments. Cole knew the poor guy would lose a lot in the big crash of 1929, but that was twelve years away. He'd had the thought earlier of warning Flynn, but, as a ghost, did he really have the capability of changing the future? If he saw Agnieszka again, he would ask her that question, although she would most likely answer with obscure riddles.

Cole felt sorry for Laurence Flynn. The man seemed to be an okay guy, and yet his wife was cheating on him and, if those ladies were to be believed, just using him for social status.

A woman not dressed in a costume entered the ballroom carrying a blonde little girl wearing a long nightgown. The child, who looked to be about three years old, had a tear-soaked red face. The woman perused the room, spotted Flynn, and crossed the floor to him.

"What have we here?" Flynn said, taking the little girl into his arms.

"She had a nightmare and wanted her daddy," the nanny said.

"Oh, Miranda, darling, I'm sorry you had a nightmare."

Her father cuddled the girl to him and stroked her head as she cried some more. "Where's mommy?" He looked around the ballroom for his wife.

The nanny said, "She insisted on seeing daddy."

"Has Theresa been up at all to see her before her bedtime?"

"No, sir."

Flynn just nodded, as if he were aware there was a problem. He lifted little Miranda's head and spoke in a funny voice. "Okay my little princess, you know that little princesses must get their beauty sleep in order to stay a pretty little princess. Otherwise you turn into a big ugly ogre with six eyes, four noses, and an elephant trunk!"

Miranda laughed, probably more at the caricature voice than at the words.

"Do you want to find mommy before you go to bed?"

The girl shook her head and then snuggled it back into her father's neck.

"Where *is* Theresa, anyway?" Flynn asked rhetorically. He told Miranda, "Mommy's busy playing hostess at the party, darling, and daddy needs to be the host. Can you go back with Rose up to your room and go to sleep now? I promise we'll do something fun tomorrow."

Miranda reluctantly nodded her head.

"Good girl." He handed her back to the nanny, who apologized for interrupting him at the party.

"It's all right, Rose. I'm always happy to see my daughter."

The nanny took Miranda away and out of the ballroom. Flynn shrugged at his friends, laughed with slight embarrassment, and said, "Ah, the joys of being a father." The men clapped him on the back and such, providing words of support and encouragement.

So, Laurence Flynn was a pretty good father, Cole thought, unlike the mother. Speaking of which, it was probably nearing the time in which Theresa Flynn would meet her destiny upstairs in one of the rooms. Cole turned, left the ballroom, and stepped into the foyer just in time to see the woman herself emerge from the ladies' room and go over to the elevators. Theresa's eyes darted around the foyer to make sure she wasn't seen. The golden doors opened, and she slipped inside. When they closed, Cole watched the floor indicator light above the elevator. The lift stopped on floor three.

Cole took off to the stairs and ran up to the next level. The third floor was quiet, the lonely hallway stretching away from the top of the staircase and the elevator bank. Theresa Flynn's back was to him as she walked quickly to a door halfway down the corridor. She knocked. The door opened and she slipped inside. Cole thought it might be Room 308 or thereabouts.

Could he stop what was about to happen? Should he even try?

Cole began to walk along the hallway and had gone only a few steps when the door to Room 302 opened. He stopped to see who was exiting, but no one was there. It was as if the open door was beckoning him to enter.

He then realized that Room 302 was the master suite—the Apartment—the one in which the Flynn family lived, the largest quarters in the entire hotel.

Weren't the nanny and little Miranda in there? Who opened the door?

He stood there a moment, perplexed.

Had the door opened…for him?

His instincts suggested that he should go inside.

8

As soon as he stepped through the open door, Cole felt a faint tremor and the lighting shifted around him. The door closed without touching it.

Daylight streamed into the apartment from windows at the end of the entry foyer where he stood. He hesitantly moved forward, wondering what the hell he had trod into. Something was very different. It had been nighttime out in the corridor.

A T-intersection in the corridor gave him a choice to go left to what appeared to be a hallway of bedroom doors. A living room was straight ahead. He peeked inside it to see a rather plain collection of furniture. The ceiling paint was peeling. A newspaper, an empty glass, and a bottle of vodka sat on a coffee table that was the focus of a sofa/comfy chair combination.

Cole moved across the room and saw that an archway to the left went to a kitchen. Piles of dirty dishes and glasses occupied the counter by the sink. A row of baby bottles and rubber nipples were drying on a towel.

He heard voices coming from deeper within the apartment, probably one of the bedrooms off the other hallway. A man and a woman. Curiously, Cole wasn't concerned about getting caught. This might be one of those times when he was invisible. And if not, well, he was dead anyway; what could anyone do to him?

Cole went to the living room window and looked out. The street below had changed. There were now many more automobiles, but still vintage models. No horses and carriages, but many yellow taxis. The cars were the kind that were in movies from the 40s. The sun shone brightly, and New Yorker pedestrians bustled along the sidewalks. At an angle, he could get a glimpse of Times Square a couple of blocks uptown. A movie theater marquee displayed the title *The Treasure of the Sierra Madre.*

When did that movie come out?

Cole realized that although he was in Room 302, the master suite of Hotel Destiny, it was no longer 1917, or 1985, for that matter.

He turned back to the room and went to the coffee table. The newspaper next to the vodka was dated July 10, 1948.

Then it all came back to him. He didn't know a tremendous amount about Hotel Destiny's infamous history, but he did know that there had been a fire—possibly caused by arson—on this floor back in the late forties. Probably that same year. The daughter of the original owner, Miranda Flynn, had perished in that fire. She had been living in this very suite. During the '70s and '80s when Cole worked in the hotel, Room 302 was never usable. It hadn't been properly restored until Marvin Trent bought the place and did the remodeling.

The voices in the back of the apartment grew a little louder. The couple was arguing, but he couldn't make out the words.

Maybe the best thing to do was to get out. There was nothing for him here, unless….

Agnieszka had mentioned that portals took him to years that were significant in his life. How could this place have anything to do with his past?

Except...although he'd been an orphan, he knew that he'd been born in 1948. His adoptive parents admitted to him once that neither they nor the orphanage knew the exact day, but it was early summer of that year. June or July.

Cole went back to the foyer, peered down the bedroom hallway and noticed that one of the doors was open. He quietly and slowly moved toward it. The quarreling man and woman were behind a closed door farther down the corridor.

"What do you expect me to do?" the man shouted. "I'm not going to live here with those bastards in the hotel!"

There was a slap and the woman cried out. Then, through sobs, she shrieked, "You're the bastard, Curly!"

Should he intervene? Who were these people?

Instead, he looked in the open bedroom. It was a nursery that contained two cribs, over which hung mobiles of plastic moons and stars. Sunlight streamed in from the windows next to one of them. Cole heard a goo-gooing sound from one of the cribs. He cautiously stepped forward.

Each crib contained a baby. The one nearest the window was awake, its little eyes wide open and focused on Cole. The other infant was asleep. From the colors of the blankets—blue—he guessed that both babies were boys. They appeared to be very young...a few days old, perhaps. They looked identical. Twins?

"Hey there," Cole whispered to the baby that was awake.

Wait a second...that baby can see me! He's responding.

Cole realized he was still wearing the damned mask and cloak. He removed the mask and revealed his full face to the baby, who continued to stare at him. The infant was too young to smile—Cole thought that babies didn't start smiling until around three months old.

He heard the bedroom door down the hall suddenly open. Cole froze as footsteps grew louder as they approached. Then, a blonde woman in her early thirties appeared in the doorway. She looked haggard, overweight, had a red cheek from the earlier slap, and smeared makeup from crying. She wore a ratty bathrobe and slippers.

"It's you again!" she gasped when she saw Cole standing by the cribs.

Me again? What does she mean by that?

He held up his hands. "I'm, uh, here by mistake. Sorry!" He started to move toward the door, but she blocked the way.

"What are you doing in here?" Then she squinted at him. "Who *are* you? Why do I keep seeing you?"

"You must have me confused with someone else." However, he knew certain truths about Room 302. "Listen to me, you need to get out of here. There's going to be a fire. A bad one. Take those kids out of here and leave."

"I can't take this anymore! Why are you doing this? *Why?* You keep...you keep showing up every few years!"

That threw him. "I do?"

"Come on, we met when I was sixteen, and then we danced

together at a New Year's party years later, and then you tried to help me when Curly was beating me. And then I saw you on the roof of the hotel this past New Year's Eve, and then they killed Michael!"

Cole didn't know what she was talking about. *Michael?*

"And...and...you were in the room right after I had my babies! Who *are* you? Why do you keep *haunting* me? You have to stop! Do you hear me? Go away!" Then she glanced over at the cribs and back at him. "Wait...what are you doing in here with the children? What do you want with them?" Her hysteria built until she hollered, "Get out of here!"

Alarmed, Cole pushed past her, nearly knocking her over. He ran to the foyer just as a loud, masculine voice behind him shouted, "Hey!" Cole reached the apartment door, tried to open it, but it wouldn't budge.

The man had made it to the T-intersection, and from the sound of his footsteps and voice, this was a very big guy.

He can't hurt me! I'm a ghost!

Still, Cole was very afraid. He wanted out of there. Struggling with the door, he realized the bolt lock was in place. He quickly slid it open, turned the knob, and he was back in the hallway of the third floor. The door to Room 302 slammed shut.

All was quiet. Again, there was the subtle shift of lighting and he felt the light tremor in the floor. He instinctively knew that it was nighttime again. In fact, as he stood there catching his breath, he came to realize that he was back where he was before he'd entered Room 302. Was it 1917 again?

Just to make sure, Cole put his ear to the door of 302 and listened. He heard nothing.

What had just happened? Who was that couple? What was the woman babbling about? She had acted like she knew him. She'd accused him of *haunting* her. What the hell?

He remembered Agnieszka's voice, telling him about the memories he might experience when traveling through the portals. *You will relive moments of your life, or, more often, be an observer of moments from your life.*

He must have gone through a portal.

Wait a second….

Room 302. A fire. 1948. The year of his birth.

Could the burn injuries on his body—that he'd had as long as he could *remember*—could they have been caused in *that* fire? In Room 302?

Don't tell me one of those babies was…me…?

At that point, the elevator dinged, and the gold doors opened. A couple in costume emerged and started walking toward him. The man held on to the woman, who was struggling to walk evenly. They were both heavily intoxicated.

"Good evening!" the man called out. "Great party, eh?"

Cole grunted an acknowledgment. He could still be seen. Then he asked, "This is 1917, right?"

The man laughed. "You must have had more to drink than us! Yes, sir, it's still 1917. My good man, I don't think that party lasted until New Year's!" The woman laughed and they moved on. "Good night!"

Keys appeared and the fellow unlocked Room 305. The couple went inside and closed the door.

Cole rubbed his eyes. Funny how one could still feel weary, even if one were dead. At least he had confirmation that he was back in 1917 where he had been before entering Room 302. The white mask was still in his hand. Instead of putting it back on his face, he stuck it in his jacket pocket.

Cole then attempted to shake off the bizarre notion that he might have just viewed himself as a newborn, and he refocused on his original goal to check on Theresa Flynn and Bradley Granger. He moved farther down the hall to Room 308, where the couple was allegedly engaged in illicit activity. As he drew closer to the door, though, he heard sounds of a struggle. Theresa was telling him *No No No*, and there was a crash of something on the floor, followed by a *Stop Stop Stop* and a *Put That Down!*

BANG!

The gunshot caused Cole to jump. He hollered, "Hey!" and pounded on the door. "Open up! Open up!"

Granger wasn't going to voluntarily open the door, so Cole stepped back, raised his right leg, and kicked the door with the sole of his shoe. The structure gave a little. He kicked it again, and the lock burst. They didn't make them as strong in those days.

The man from Room 305 opened his door, looked out of his room, and called out, "What's happening? Is everything all right down there?"

Cole rushed into 308 to find the tragedy he'd expected. Theresa Flynn, dressed only in torn undergarments, lay on the bed. Her chest was a mess of blood red. Bradley Granger sat on the edge of the bed, a pistol in hand. His face was one of abject horror at what he'd done.

"It...it was an accident!" he pleaded.

Cole commanded, "Put down the gun, Mr. Granger. I'm the hotel detective."

"We were...playing a game, and I wanted to...I didn't mean to...."

"Drop the gun! Now!"

Granger jumped up with a cry of anguish and started to wave his weapon as if it were a flag. Cole jumped at him, grabbed the man's gun-arm with both hands, and the pair grappled for control of it. Granger attempted to point the barrel at Cole, but the man was too distraught and drunk to be too effective. Cole bent Granger's arm at the elbow, but the man just wouldn't drop the pistol. Still clutching the actor's forearm, Cole slammed his own elbow into Granger's nose.

BANG!

Granger flopped backwards onto the bed and halfway on top of Theresa Flynn. The weapon had discharged in the actor's face.

Cole's immediate thought was, *He ain't a matinee idol no more!*

But then his next consideration was...*Did Bradley Granger really kill himself, or did I do it?*

"Shit," he said.

Granger still held the gun in his hand. It would appear to any investigator that this was a murder-suicide.

Cole backed out of the room—the door was still open, the lock busted—and found himself surrounded by policemen. Four uniformed officers slipped past him into the room while a photographer took pictures of the crime scene. Bulbs flashed brightly, capturing in one's retinas silver still images of the carnage. Laurence Flynn stood with his back against the hallway wall. He appeared to be very upset and his face was pale. A plainclothes detective spoke to him softly.

How did all of them get here so quickly? Cole was very confused.

"I saw it happen," he said to the detective. "Granger shot himself!"

But no one heard him. He was invisible again.

Agnieszka words came back to him. *Time will play games with you, no matter where you are or when you are. It can sometimes be like an edit in a film.* He had just experienced a "jump cut." Time had progressed by an hour or two since the deaths, and now the police were there.

There was nothing more he could do there. Cole moved away from the crime scene, past hotel guests who were kept behind a taped-off area of the hallway. Cole ducked under the tape and approached the elevator bank and Grand Stairs. A familiar-looking woman stood at the head `of the staircase. She was dressed in a costume resembling Marie Antoinette.

Theresa Flynn.

She was motionless, staring at Cole. Shell-shocked, perhaps. The expression on her face indicated that she was having trouble accepting the fact that she was now dead.

Theresa had been a beautiful, vibrant woman. Wife and mother. Adulteress. Victim of foul play. Now she was a ghost.

Cole rang for the elevator instead of having to walk past her to descend the stairs.

Once he was on the first floor, things changed once again. This was the lobby he had come to know while working at the hotel during the 1970s and early '80s. Run down, sleazy, and unfriendly. It was daylight, but it was snowing outside. By taking the elevator, he had obviously slipped through another portal.

He recognized a woman named Crystal at the reception desk. She had been employed at the hotel in the late '70s but left after a year or so. Cole couldn't remember the exact dates, but he did know what he would find back in his office, so that's where he went.

The place was very familiar. All the things he knew were there. If he wasn't mistaken...Cole opened the top left drawer of his desk and found his Smith & Wesson handgun and the precious pint of Jack Daniel's. He had always tried to keep it in stock. Cole pulled out the bottle and took a long, satisfying swig of the fiery brown liquid. He then took off the stupid black cloak, removed the white mask from his jacket pocket, and threw it all on the floor.

He went to the mirror and examined his face. Bloodshot eyes. A sickly pallor. An expression of apathy and sadness.

Cole wasn't sure if he'd learned anything so far except that maybe...*maybe...* he had once been a baby in the hotel. Was the blonde woman he'd seen in Room 302 his mother?

It was clear that there was more to discover in Hotel Destiny.

9

Cole sat in the office and drank whiskey for a while. It was like the old days when he was alive and had a job at Hotel Destiny as the night manager and hotel detective. He tried to imagine where his living self would be at this moment in time in the late '70s. Home in bed? Probably, since it was currently daylight. He had tended to work mostly nights. Once he was married to Janine in 1980, that was usually the case as well. She hadn't liked it. Janine kept non-vampire hours by working during the day as a secretary in a financial firm while he slept. They were ships passing in the night, together for just a little while each night and morning before the other person went off to work.

Glancing at the clock that had been on his desk forever, he saw that it was getting to be the dinner hour. Oddly, he hadn't felt hunger or thirst—for water, that is—since he'd died. Agnieszka had said he'd feel certain things like living people, but so far, he had been unaware of any pangs of that sort. Thank goodness alcohol still worked! If that had been ineffective, then this existence would truly be hell.

For a moment he thought that staying a ghost in the hotel forever might not be such a bad deal. No one was bothering him. If he could figure out how to become visible at will, then he might be able to amuse himself with the guests. He'd eventually have to find another place in the building to serve as his hangout, seeing that Marvin Trent was soon going to remodel the administrative offices. If he had lived and retained employment, Cole wouldn't have been allowed to keep a makeshift bedroom in the adjacent space.

Nevertheless, the mystery was bugging him. Cole didn't

understand the metaphysics of what was going on. He hadn't believed in an afterlife, a god, a heaven or a hell, or anything of that sort prior to his murder. He'd thought that when one died, it was over. Death was like what one's perception was prior to birth. You weren't aware of your existence because you didn't exist.

And yet, here he was. A supernatural being who could time travel. Sure, he still needed to work out the nuts and bolts and learn how to properly navigate this extraordinary phenomenon, but at least he wasn't a blank slate with no consciousness.

Well, you're not going to educate yourself sitting here getting drunk.

He managed to stand and put away the bottle. He didn't know what he would do when it was empty. Steal from the kitchen, he supposed. Some poor busboy would probably get the blame as more and more bottles of alcohol went missing over time.

Cole walked out of the office. Crystal was still at the front desk. As he walked past her, she said, "Oh, Mr. Sackler! I didn't know you were here!"

Ah. He was visible again. "Uh, yeah, I came into the office today. Didn't mean to freak you out."

Crystal laughed a little. "Doesn't take much to freak me out in this place." She shook her head. "I'm glad you're here. I think there's some drug dealing going on, seventh floor."

Cole searched his brain to try and remember the events of those late '70s. One notorious criminal had made Hotel Destiny his headquarters for a while. "Byron Chavez? Is he up there?"

"Yes, sir. Shall I call the police?"

"Nah. I'll take care of it."

He had no intention of doing so. He'd let his living self do it, which is most likely what he had done back in the day. There had been more arrests than he could count. Drug dealers, junkies, hookers and johns, sellers of stolen and/or illegal goods…whatever shouldn't be done legitimately was performed at Hotel Destiny in those days. For most of the time during the hotel's sleazy period, management had turned a blind eye. No one else was renting rooms except the riff raff. New York Street Skunk.

The serial murders were a different story. If he could have stopped them, he would have.

Cole crossed the lobby and decided to take the elevator instead of the stairs. There was a portal in the lift, right? The last time he had ridden in it, the time had changed.

Let's test that theory....

He stepped into the decrepit old thing, pushed the button for floor two, and off he went. When the doors opened, the ballroom foyer indeed appeared to be different than it was in the '70s. There was still an elegance to it, although signs of deterioration had begun. There was a sense of decay that hadn't quite set in.

A black maid ran a vintage Hoover vacuum machine over the carpet. It coughed and sputtered as she attempted to pick up the dust.

"Pardon me, ma'am?"

The woman looked up. "Yes, sir?"

She sees and hears me! "How old is that machine?"

"This here Hoover?"

"Yes, ma'am."

"It's a few months old. Mr. Flynn purchased it just before the Crash."

"You mean, in 1929?"

"Yes, sir."

Cole rubbed his chin. "How many months ago was that Crash? Time flies so quickly...."

"Six months, sir. Winter's over. We're finally getting some spring weather, aren't we, sir."

Cole nodded. "Yes. Thank you."

So, now it was April 1930. Interesting. Why did he step into this particular year?

He heard piano music drifting out of the ballroom doors. He stepped to them and peered inside. The place was dismantled, between events. Round dining tables covered the floor, but the chairs were stacked upside down on top of them. No tablecloths. The bar was shut down, bottles of booze nowhere in sight. In 1930, Prohibition was in effect. What a disaster!

A young woman—a teenager, really—was on stage playing

the grand piano. She was blonde and wore a yellow dress. Cole didn't know the music. It was something classical. The girl wasn't a very good player, but she wasn't a bad one. She'd had some lessons.

He went up to the edge of the stage. Once he was closer, he could see that she was a younger, smaller, and much thinner version of the haggard lady he'd seen in Room 302 in 1948 with the twin babies. Here, though, she was at the cusp of womanhood—fresh, pretty, and spruced.

When she saw him, she quit and pulled her hands away from the keys.

"Don't stop on my account," he said. "It sounds good."

She shook her head. "Thank you, but no, it's terrible. I had to quit my lessons."

"How come?"

"Why do you think? Daddy lost so much money last October. He can barely hold on to this place." She gestured to the room with a sweep of her hand.

"Your...your father is Laurence Flynn?"

"Uh huh." She cocked her head at him. "Are you a guest at the hotel?"

"I am."

Her blue eyes widened. "We don't get too many guests these days. I hope you're enjoying your stay."

"It's very nice, thank you."

So, this was Miranda Flynn. Cole quickly did the math. If she had been three in 1917, then she was....

"Are you, what, about sixteen years old?" he asked.

"Yes. My name is Miranda, what's yours?"

"Cole."

"Nice to meet you. Are you going to some fancy party?"

"I beg your pardon?"

"You're all dressed up."

Cole looked down and winced. Although he had removed the cloak and mask, he was still wearing a tuxedo. "I was out all night and haven't changed. By all means, do keep playing. I didn't mean to disturb you. I'll leave you alone." He started to walk away.

"No, don't go." She turned on the piano bench to face him. "It's pretty lonely here. Most of the time I'm here in this big place with just the ghosts to keep me company." She laughed a little.

Cole shot her a look. "Ghosts?"

"You think I'm joking, but there are ghosts in this place."

"Really?"

"There sure are."

"Tell me about them."

"You think I'm being silly. That's what my father says."

"I don't think you're silly. I believe in ghosts."

"You do?"

"I do. What have you…seen?"

She seemed encouraged by his interest. "Well, I've seen three different ones. I think the one I've seen the most is a man who wears a black cloak and a white mask."

That made Cole swallow. "Where do you see him?"

"Different places. In here. Up on the third floor, where my father and I live. I don't remember where else."

"Do you talk to him?"

"No. I shut my eyes, and then when I open them again, he's gone. He doesn't scare me, though. He's a little creepy because he looks like the Phantom of the Opera with that mask on. Did you see that movie with Lon Chaney?"

"Yes." Cole rubbed his chin. "Who else do you see?"

"The others are pretty awful. They scare me. I once saw a man whose head was all bloody. Part of his face was gone." She shuddered. "It was terrible. I screamed."

"Where was this?"

"On the third floor, in the hallway."

"That sounds frightening. Anyone else?"

She looked down and pursed her lips. "Sometimes I see… my mother."

"Your mother?"

Miranda nodded. "She died when I was three, but I recognize her from pictures." She pointed to the wall where the paintings had hung. Now only Laurence Flynn's portrait was there. "There used to be a painting of her over there next to my father's. He had it removed and stored it in the basement. We still have some photographs. She was very pretty."

"Where do you see her?"

"Also on the third floor. You'd think there's some kind of party of the dead going on there. Ghosts everywhere!" She laughed.

"Does she speak to you?"

Miranda shook her head. "No. I spoke to her once. I asked her if she was my mother. She turned and sort of flew away, kind of disappeared into the shadows."

"Does she frighten you?"

"No. She looks too sad to be frightening. I think she's very unhappy. Given what happened to her...." Miranda turned away. "I'm sorry, Cole, I don't know how much you know about my mother."

"It's all right, Miranda. I know. You don't have to tell me more. Look, I'm going to let you continue your practicing. Thank you for talking to me."

"All right. Have a nice evening."

Cole turned and made his way across the ballroom as the girl started in on Beethoven's "Moonlight Sonata."

When he had seen Miranda in 1948 in Room 302, she had said that they had met when she was sixteen. Was this the reason? Had she remembered seeing his *ghost* in 1930?

Bizarre.

This time he took the stairs down to the lobby. Lining the wall there were framed photographs he'd never seen before. The 1920s had apparently been very good to the hotel. The "jazz years" were bountiful all over America, even though Prohibition had put a damper on public socializing. Cole guessed that Hotel Destiny had ways of supplying alcohol to its guests, though, the same way all elite establishments did. The pictures displayed the likes of Harpo Marx, George S. Kaufman, Marion Davies, Mae West, and even Herbert Hoover. Laurence Flynn was in many of the photos. The death of his wife and the ensuing scandal had not hurt the reputation of the hotel. On the contrary, it had probably helped it.

As if on cue, Flynn emerged from the offices behind the

reception desk. He was with a distinguished-looking lawyer-type, who was saying, "… not to worry, Laurence. We can always sell the hotel as a last resort, but in the meantime perhaps the economy will recover."

"I can't help but worry," Flynn said. "The so-called Roaring Twenties fizzled. Instead of going out like a lion, it was more like the braying of a sheep."

The man shook Flynn's hand. "We'll talk soon. Don't despair."

The hotelier watched the man leave the building, and then he turned and noticed Cole. "Hello," he said. "Are you a guest at the hotel?"

Cole had nothing to lose. "Yes, sir."

Flynn approached him and spoke softly. "Would you care to have a drink with me, sir?" When Cole raised an eyebrow, the man added, "I keep some of the stuff hidden in my office. I assume you're not a policeman."

"No, I'm not. I'd be delighted to have a drink with you, Mr. Flynn."

"Oh, you know me?"

"I do."

"And you are…?"

"Coleman Sackler." They shook hands, and Cole followed Flynn to the back.

10

The hotel manager always had a fancier office than Cole ever did. It was roomy, had an adjacent space for meetings, and a view of the street, which beat looking at a brick wall.

Flynn, who was now in his early forties, had aged for the worse. This was a man who might be mistaken to be in his mid-fifties. He was gaunt and didn't look healthy. His hair had turned completely gray. From what Cole had heard in the lobby, it was apparent that Flynn had lost a lot of money in the stock market crash.

"Have a seat, Mr. Sackler." Flynn gestured to a comfy chair in front of his desk. "I keep the good stuff in my safe." The man squatted to twist the knob and enter the combination numbers on the large safe that stood against the wall. Once it was open, he pulled out a bottle of Canadian Club and procured two glasses. He poured and then handed one to Cole. "I have to get it from a contact over the border. Hard times, these. You'd think the government would realize that and repeal the Twenty-first Amendment. People need to drink." Flynn lightly tapped his own glass against Cole's and said, "Cheers," and then went behind his desk to sit.

Cole sipped the delicious nectar and thanked his benefactor.

"You're welcome. I really don't like to drink alone, but I often have to." Flynn seemed to savor his liquor as much as Cole. After a long drink, the man closed his eyes and enjoyed the sensation. Then he asked, "Mr. Sackler, when did you check in to the hotel?"

"Oh, just yesterday. I won't be here long."

"Where are you from?"

Cole had to make something up. "New Jersey."

"You've got on awfully fancy clothing. Is that what they're wearing across the Hudson River on a casual basis?"

Here we go again. I really need to find some different clothes.

"Oh, I was at a wedding this morning. Just hadn't changed yet. I don't know, wearing a tux makes me feel important, I guess."

Flynn studied Cole for a moment. "Have we ever met before, Mr. Sackler?"

"Well, believe it or not, I was at the hotel's gala opening party."

The hotelier's brow creased. "On Halloween?"

"Yes, sir. 1917."

"You were here?"

"Yes."

A dark shadow passed over Flynn's face. Obviously, what happened that night was still painful for him.

Cole looked away, now uncomfortable. Several moments passed. A clock in the office ticked away.

"It was a difficult night," Flynn finally said. "I thought the scandal would ruin me. Surprisingly, the past decade was very good for the hotel. I could never remarry, though. Believe me, I could have had my pick of many women who threw themselves at me. Even a couple of film stars. I suppose it might have been better for my daughter if I had. Did you know I have a daughter?"

"Yes. Miranda."

Flynn nodded. "She's in the hotel somewhere. She has the run of the place. I might have to sell it, Mr. Sackler. My attorney was just here. He's going to make a last-ditch effort to find some investors to help pull me out of the red. I don't have much faith in that."

"I'm sorry to hear that," Cole said. Even though he was a misanthrope at heart, Cole didn't think this man deserved the bad fortune he had received. It just went to show how awful life could be, that no one was immune to pain and sorrow.

"Do you know Edgar Allan Poe?" Flynn asked.

"Not personally."

Flynn smiled at the joke, but then grew serious again. "He

wrote a poem that I often find relevant. It's called 'Spirits of the Dead.' Do you know it?"

"I'm afraid not."

The man began to recite.

Thy soul shall find itself alone
'Mid dark thoughts of the gray tombstone—
Not one, of all the crowd, to pry
Into thine hour of secrecy.
Be silent in that solitude,
Which is not loneliness—for then
The spirits of the dead who stood
In life before thee are again
In death around thee—and their will
Shall overshadow thee: be still.
The night, tho' clear, shall frown—
And the stars shall look not down
From their high thrones in the heaven,
With light like Hope to mortals given—
But their red orbs, without beam,
To thy weariness shall seem
As a burning and a fever
Which would cling to thee for ever.
Now are thoughts thou shalt not banish.
Now are visions ne'er to vanish;
From thy spirit shall they pass
No more—like dew-drop from the grass.
The breeze—the breath of God—is still
And the mist upon the hill,
Shadowy—shadowy—yet unbroken,
Is a symbol and a token—
How it hangs upon the trees,
A mystery of mysteries!

Flynn was silent then. He stared at the glass of whiskey in his hand.

Cole needed to get out of there. *And I thought I was depressed...!* He shifted in his seat and took a last swallow of the whiskey.

"Would you do me a favor, Mr. Sackler?" the hotelier asked.

"Sure."

Flynn opened a drawer and removed a revolver. It wasn't a Smith & Wesson, like Cole's, but rather a Colt .38 Police Positive. The man flipped open the cylinder and checked to see that it was loaded to the brim. He snapped it shut and held it out to Cole.

"Would you be so kind as to shoot me in the head?"

"*What?*"

"I'm too much of a coward to do it myself. Please? You could easily get away. There's an exit through that door." He pointed to the adjoining room.

"Mr. Flynn, no, I'm not going to do that." Cole stood and set the empty glass on the desk. "Thank you for the drink. I appreciate it. I think I need to leave now."

"Forgive me, Mr. Sackler. I should not have said that. I am not myself lately." The man set the gun on his desk. "You don't need to go."

Cole hesitated at the office door. "Mr. Flynn, may I make a suggestion?"

The man merely nodded.

Cole moved to the desk and picked up the gun. He opened the cylinder and removed all the cartridges. He laid all six out on top of the desk. "Now, watch." He picked up one cartridge, inserted it into a chamber, spun the cylinder, shut it, and handed it back to Flynn. "Make it a game, sir. It's more fun that way. I do it all the time."

Flynn looked at him. "Russian Roulette? You 'do it all the time'?"

"Lately, yes. What's life but a gamble anyway?"

Flynn stared at Cole for a moment and then smiled. "That's a great idea."

Cole considered telling the man that things were bound to get better, but he knew the truth. "Thanks again for the drink."

He left, walked to the lobby, and climbed the staircase to the second floor. Was Miranda still playing the piano? Would it do any good to tell her that her father was contemplating suicide?

A pretty, dark-haired maid exited the ballroom before he could enter. Cole did a double-take, for she was none other than Agnieszka! The woman ignored Cole and went straight to the passage that accessed the hotel's kitchen.

"Agnieszka!" he called.

He hurried to follow her, went into the small corridor and through the swinging doors, and he was in the kitchen. Nothing much was happening. A black cook sat and read the newspaper, waiting for a room service order. He looked up and saw Cole, who asked, "Did you see a maid walk through here?"

The cook shook his head. "Are you a guest of the hotel? You shouldn't be in here, sir."

Cole didn't answer. He rushed past the preparation counters, refrigerators, and stoves, and into another employees-only area where food storage was located.

There. Agnieszka was opening the big pantry. She stepped inside, and the door closed behind her. Cole ran to the pantry, opened it, and stared into a dark, featureless space that wasn't in the least inviting. He hesitated a moment.

Oh, what the hell....

Cole stepped inside, was engulfed by blackness, and the pantry door slammed shut behind him.

11

For a moment, Cole felt as if he had returned to that void he had experienced directly after his murder. Nothingness. No sound or light. He wasn't sure if he was standing on solid flooring or not.

Then—flames erupted around him! Huge, whipping sheets of heat, burning the space with yellow and red and orange terror. The smoke was gray and thick, and Cole couldn't breathe.

He was desperately afraid of fire. If there was one dread he'd had for his entire life, it was pyrophobia. He wore the scars on his left leg, hip, and side to prove it. Cole couldn't remember when he had been burned by fire; it had occurred when he was a small child, perhaps not even one year old. His adoptive parents didn't know the circumstances or when it had happened, only that he had miraculously survived. After his encounter in Room 302 in the bedroom with the two cribs, he had begun to wonder if the trauma had occurred *at* the hotel.

There was no place to move. Cole smelled his skin burning and felt the agony of scorching, blistering terror.

Agnieszka had said that he would experience pain but that he couldn't be physically harmed.

Fuck that!

He screamed. He thrashed and searched for a way out of the inferno.

Was he in hell now? Had the "experiment" as a ghost completely failed? Had he been sent here for the rest of eternity?

God, no!

Cole dropped to his knees and attempted to pray, even though he had given up praying when he was a teen. It had never done anything for him, but by God, he was going to try it again now!

He shut his eyes tightly, and the heat abruptly dissipated.

Cole gasped. The relief was tangible. The quality of air around him changed and he could breathe fresh, clear oxygen.

He opened his eyes...and he was in that dark, stretching corridor that contained framed photos from his life. He was back where he had started.

Cole stood and examined himself. His tuxedo was not burned or seared. His exposed skin was fine.

I really have to get out of this goddamned tux.

With a sigh, Cole turned to look at the photo that hung on the "wall" next to him. It showed a playroom for small children. There were toys, a couple of balls, baby swings, and spilled building blocks on the floor. The POV was just a few inches up, as if seen by a crawling infant.

What the...?

Then he heard the distant sound of babies crying. The noise came from another draped archway up ahead to the right. Curiosity got the better of him, so he moved forward. Perhaps this would be another clue to follow in this strange journey to find his fucking "heritage."

Cole stepped through the archway and found himself alone in the very same playroom that was in the photo. The place was the size of a grade-school classroom. Daylight streamed in through windows. He scanned the view and figured the street outside resembled somewhere in New York City, but he didn't recognize it. He didn't think it was Manhattan. Brooklyn, perhaps? Queens? Something about it was familiar. Cars parked along the curb were the same vintage he had seen in 1948. The year couldn't be much different from that.

This is a memory. A place in my head, but I'm really still in the hotel. Right?

He didn't think he'd ever seen this playroom before, though, unless he had been too young to remember it.

Two swinging doors with windows stood at one end. He went to peer through them and saw a hallway and a couple of open doors to what appeared to be offices. The corridor jogged to the left.

Three people emerged from around the corner and walked

to one of the open doors—a woman dressed in late 1940s- or early 50s-era business attire, and a husband and wife who were likely in their thirties.

Oh, Christ....

The couple was Fred and Florence Sackler, his adoptive parents. They were young and vibrant, but they seemed to be a little nervous.

Cole opened the swinging doors and stepped out. No one could see him. He was invisible again.

"… here at Green Garden Orphanage we do our best to place the children with the most appropriate parents," the businesswoman was saying.

Green Garden Orphanage! My parents had told me that was where they adopted me from! It was in Queens!

As an adult he had attempted to go there to see if he could find out anything about his birth parents, but the place had closed sometime in the early '70s. No wonder the street outside had looked vaguely familiar.

"My wife is a little concerned about the burn wounds," Fred Sackler said. "So am I, frankly."

The administrator paused before leading them into her office. "The twins were burned in the fire, as I told you. Little Charles, the poor thing, suffered more severe injuries. However, we have been assured that the burns little Coleman endured are not life threatening. He will heal and live a productive life. Recovery from the skin grafting will take time, so right now, yes, they don't look too good. As they heal, the skin will be patchy in those places. I'm not going to lie to you. He will always have the scars throughout his life. But unless he wears short pants, no one will see them as he grows up."

Florence Sackler turned to her husband. "I would like to see him, Fred."

"Of course, dear."

"I was hoping you would say that," the administrator said. "He's only four months old, young enough, that is, if you wanted to change his name from Coleman."

"I rather like that name," Florence said.

"Come inside here to my office. We need to fill out some

paperwork, and then I'll take you to the nursery where he's napping."

The trio went through the door and it shut behind them. Cole moved to it, wanting to hear more. As soon as he touched the knob, though, the flames returned. The fire engulfed everything around him, encircling him, coming ever closer. The smoke was heavy and made him cough and choke.

He felt a burning sensation as the eight-foot-tall blaze threatened to suck him in. There was a pull on his body, as if the fire wanted to consume him. Cole thrust himself backwards, away from what seemed to be the source of the conflagration.

Cole fell on his rear and back onto hard checkerboard tiling. Bright lights nearly blinded him, and he yelped.

The fire was gone. He was back in Hotel Destiny's kitchen. In front of him was the pantry door that he had attempted to go through earlier. The one Agnieszka had disappeared into.

Cole looked around him. The cook stood a few feet away.

"Are you all right, mister?"

"What happened?" Cole asked.

"You tried to go into the pantry, but you fainted."

"I was…unconscious?"

"Yes, sir. For a few seconds. I was just coming over to see if you were okay."

He had gone into a Dream State. Why were these occurring so often again?

Cole slowly got to his feet. He didn't seem to be hurt. "I'm all right, thanks."

"Are you sure? I could call the house doctor."

"No, no. I'll be…. Say, do you know the maid? Agnieszka?"

"Who?"

"She's a maid at the hotel. Agnieszka. She's from Poland."

The cook shook his head. "Sorry, sir, there's no maid I know of here named that, and I know all the maids."

Cole nodded. The only explanation was that he must be in a time period before Agnieszka was employed at the hotel. The figure he'd seen go into the "pantry," or whatever it was, had to have been her ghost.

"I'll get out of your way now," he said, and then he made his way out of the kitchen and into the ballroom foyer.

Cole couldn't get the image of Fred and Florence Sackler out of his head.

So, it was true. He *had* been a twin. Charles—Charlie—had also been burned, but much worse than he had. So how long did it take for *Charlie* to be adopted? The day he had just witnessed from his past, when his parents had adopted him, may have been the last time he had seen his brother.

All those years he had *pretended*, he had *imagined*, he had *created* a "fantasy" brother...but Charlie really existed after all.

12

Cole descended the Grand Stairs and entered the lobby. Something was different. Several stacks of taped-up boxes stood on the floor. No one manned the registration desk. The lights were off. The only illumination came in from the windows, and it was a gray, cold, rainy day.

Miranda Flynn sat in one of the lobby chairs, dressed as if she were about to go somewhere. An overcoat lay across her lap and a suitcase stood beside her chair. There was a folded newspaper on top of the suitcase. Miranda appeared to be tired, or perhaps unhappy about something, but only a little older than she was the last time he had seen her.

An older man sat in the chair next to hers. Cole figured that he was in his late thirties, maybe early forties. He was a large guy. Someone you wouldn't want to mess with. He had a crewcut and was wearing a jacket and tie. He, too, had an overcoat draped over his lap.

The man was leaning forward, apparently attempting to comfort Miranda for some reason. Their body language indicated that the couple was more than friends.

"No one blames you, Miranda," the man said. "It's perfectly understandable that you had to declare bankruptcy and close the hotel temporarily. That's the key word here, Miranda—*temporary*. I know you're still mourning, but your father did a lousy thing. Leaving you with the bill the way he did was not very considerate."

"Keep my father out of it, Curly. He was so despondent. He never recovered after my mother was killed. Even though the hotel did well for several years, he was terribly melancholic. Then, with the stock market crash and everything...."

"Oh, I know, Miranda, dear, he experienced a lot of tragedy. What I'm saying is no one blames you. Your creditors are being reasonable, although personally I'd like to cut off their fingers."

Hearing that, Cole knew the man's identity. James "Curly" Chadwick. The mobster and racketeer who had managed Hotel Destiny in the thirties and forties. Like most gangsters of the time, he had built a reputation as a bootlegger during Prohibition, but after the repeal he got into the usual organized crime activities—gambling, prostitution, protection rackets, and narcotics. His outfit, made up of men of English, Scottish, and Irish extraction, competed with the more well-known Italian mafia families.

Neither Miranda nor Chadwick noticed Cole. The toggling between being visible and not was driving him nuts. Just minutes ago, he was able to converse with the cook in the kitchen. Now he was just a ghost.

Cole moved closer to the couple. As he eavesdropped, he checked out the newspaper. It had been folded with an inner page on top. A headline over a small column story declared: HOTEL DESTINY TO CLOSE. The article stated that the hotel had lost revenue after the suicide of its owner, Laurence Flynn, in January. The paper was dated March 1931. That meant Miranda was now seventeen, although she looked much older and more worldly. Cole chalked that up to living through the suicide of her father, as well as being a companion to a gangster.

"Whatever made my father want to play Russian Roulette, for heaven's sake?" Miranda said with a little anger in her voice.

"I don't know," Chadwick answered. "Pretty crazy thing to do. I wonder how long he'd been doing it before the hammer fell on the unlucky chamber."

"That revolver of his was always in his desk. Once I caught him doing it. He didn't know I was standing in the doorway to his office. I watched him pull the trigger with the gun to his head. I screamed and he was very distraught that I'd seen him. That was last summer!"

"You didn't tell me that."

"I pleaded with him to never do it again. Instead of saying that he wouldn't, he told me that I shouldn't worry about him."

"I remember he was drinking a lot in those days, too. But how do the cops know he was playing Russian Roulette? Maybe he shot himself on purpose."

"There were no other bullets in the chamber, Curly. The police detective deduced that's what Dad had been doing. Most people load the gun completely, even though they know it's only going to take one bullet to kill them. And he did it *on purpose.* He had to have known there was a chance he'd be killed."

Damn! Flynn was playing Russian Roulette when he died?

Cole grimaced, for it had been his idea for Flynn to try it. Now Cole wondered why the hell he'd told the man to do so. The old cynicism that was an integral part of Cole's personality had indirectly led to the hotelier's death. He felt awful.

"Look, Miranda," Chadwick said, "I'm going to help you get solvent again. We're going to re-open the hotel. It'll take a few months, but I promise you we'll be back within a year. Now, come on, let's get out of here and go to the house in Jersey. You'll like it there. I'll make sure you're taken care of. You're my sweetheart, and that's what I'm going to do. You'll see."

"Oh, Curly, I don't know why you like me. I'm not old enough for you...."

"Yes, you are. Nobody has to know how old you are. Come on, let's go. Shake is waiting for us in the car outside."

Ew. She's seventeen and he's at least twenty years older.

Was that legal? Cole didn't think so. He wasn't clear on what the laws of consent were in New York at the time, but still....

Curly Chadwick stood and held out a hand. Miranda took it and resigned herself to getting up. They both put on their coats. Chadwick picked up her suitcase and newspaper.

"Leave the paper," she said. "I don't want it."

He shrugged and dropped it on one of the chairs. They then went to the front doors, stepped outside, and Miranda locked up. She opened her purse and dropped the keys inside.

Cole moved to the glass doors and watched through the window as Chadwick opened the back door of a vintage Ford for Miranda. Once the two of them were inside, the driver pulled the car away from the hotel.

He was alone in a closed, abandoned hotel.

Now what?

Not particularly wanting to stay in a dark, dusty hotel by himself, Cole thought he'd go to his office, enter the clothes closet, and use the portal there to go to another time. At least he thought that would work. He made his way around the reception desk and past Flynn's office, the door of which was open.

Laurence Flynn sat in a chair, holding a gun to his head. He squeezed the trigger.

Click.

The man then released the cylinder, spun it, snapped it shut, and raised it to his head again.

Click.

"You can stop doing that, now," Cole said aloud. "You're dead."

Flynn didn't hear or see him.

Cylinder, spin, snap.

Click.

"Stop!"

Cylinder, spin, snap.

Click.

It was as if Flynn was in a never-ending loop.

Cole shook his head and moved on, but he halted in his tracks when he saw Theresa Flynn standing at the end of the hallway that led to his own office. As before, her face was vacant, in shock, unbelieving that she was a lost soul.

Slowly, she raised her right hand and held it out to Cole, as if beckoning him to take it.

That's when he put it together. He'd been dense up to now. The memories he'd been witnessing had spelled it all out for him.

Miranda Flynn was his real mother. In 1948, Miranda had come running into Room 302's nursery in full protective mode, even after a fight with the man Cole now knew was Curly Chadwick. The twins were her children.

That made Laurence and Theresa Flynn his grandparents.

"Grandmother?" he whispered.

The corners of the woman's mouth jerked and twitched, as if she were trying to smile. Finally, she achieved it. It was an awkward, asymmetrical, open-mouthed excuse for a grin. It made her look hideous.

Then the blood trickled out of her mouth and ran down her chin.

Cole screamed, turned, and ran the opposite direction. He kept going past the reception desk, into the lobby, and to the elevator. He punched a button—luckily, the car was already there. He got in, blindly pushed a button, and rode the lift until it stopped.

The doors opened and Cole stumbled out, still shaking from the revelation and the horror of confronting his grandmother's ghost.

The hallway was a mess of discarded garbage and a lack of professional cleaning. Rock music on a radio could be heard coming from one of the rooms. It was contemporary stuff, the so-called "New Wave"—Talking Heads or some such band. "Burning Down the House."

Was he back in the 1980s?

It was nighttime and the lighting in the hall was poor. Some of the light fixtures were out. Yes, this was often the condition of the hotel floors in the early '80s while Cole was night manager and hotel detective.

Something compelled him to venture forward. Where was he? Numbers on the doors answered that question.

This is the sixth floor.

He knew what he was about to find. *This* memory was all too recent.

Room 605.

He didn't want to look, but something compelled him to carry it through. His memories *wanted* him to experience them again, however strange that was. It was almost as if his reminiscences had a hive mind of their own and they were controlling his journey.

The door was ajar, so he pushed it open.

The nude body of streetwalker Martine Crawford, a twenty-six-year-old black woman who had fallen on hard times in recent years, lay on the floor. Her brains had been blown away with a gun. Blood covered the carpet.

Sergeant Redenius was there with two other cops.

This had occurred on Valentine's Day 1985. It was the most recent murder in Hotel Destiny.

"And where were *you*, Sackler?" Redenius said, turning to see him in the doorway. "How many of these bodies are we going to find in your goddamned hotel while you're supposed to be in charge of security?"

Cole could barely find his voice. "I…I didn't…I was…."

Redenius held up a hand. "I know. You were drunk on your ass."

The policeman was right. He'd been totally out of it from half a bottle of Jack Daniel's. He had been in his office on the ground floor, his head on the desk, asleep, passed out. The call came that the police were on the sixth floor. In an unkempt stupor, he had managed to make his way there to meet the cops and view the ghastly sight in the room.

This can't be happening again!

Cole bolted from the crime scene and ran to the elevator bank. The Talking Heads music faded into a misty dream as the doors opened. He stepped inside and pushed the button for the second floor. Seeing Martine Crawford's corpse had unnerved him, much more so now than it had when he'd seen it in February '85. His heart pounded in his chest.

The lift stopped and the doors opened. He stormed into the second-floor foyer just in time to see a man in a black cloak and white mask on the other side of the space entering the men's restroom there.

"Hey!" Cole shouted.

Was it him? The same guy he'd seen before? Cole was sure of it. The man who had *murdered* him.

Cole hurried across the foyer and stepped into the alcove leading to the men's washroom. The lights were off, but there was enough illumination that he could just see where he was going. No one was in there. Cole went to each stall and pushed open the doors. Empty. He stood in the middle of the restroom, turned, and saw himself in the mirrors above the sink.

He was alone. "Where are you?" he asked aloud. "I saw you come in here!"

Then he spotted the door to the supply closet at one end of the bathroom. He knew it was where cleaning materials were kept, but had the man slipped inside to hide? Cole moved to it, turned the knob, and opened the door.

Nothing there but a mop and bucket, a plumber's helper, and other tools. The closet seemed to be deeper than he remembered, though. It was large enough to step into, so he did.

It was as if the baseboard was never there. Cole fell into an open, black space.

13

The sensation was *horrible*.

It was like being in one of those stomach-churning amusement-park rides that lift passengers very high off the ground and then drop them quickly. Here, though, there was no seat, no light, and no *bottom*.

Cole screamed and flailed as he continued to fall through darkness. It went on and on and on…until his consciousness faded…and drifted…

…into his memories….

He was suddenly in a little boy's bedroom. That was evident by the toys scattered haphazardly on the floor, and baseball pennants stuck on a wall. Sunlight streamed in through a window. Cole stood by a twin bed and saw that a small kid was sitting on the floor and playing with plastic dinosaurs. The door to the room was ajar.

It was all vaguely familiar, but then spotting the Mickey Mouse bedspread clinched it. Cole had had one when he was….

My God, that's me.

The boy was maybe five years old. Little Cole Sackler.

And in a blink of a second, Cole was looking out of the boy's eyes. He watched as his hand—a five-year-old hand—reached out to pick up a brontosaurus.

"My bront-o-saurus will eat your tyr-an-no-saurus," he heard himself say in a tiny voice.

Another child was in the room next to him. A mirror image of himself. A twin the same age. He, too, was playing with plastic dinosaurs. He had a tyrannosaurus rex in his hand.

"Nuh-uh, brontosauruses can't eat tyrannosauruses!" the other boy said. "My tyrannosaurus will eat your brontosaurus!"

"Charlie! No. My bront-a-saurus has big teeth to eat you."

"Cole?" came a woman's voice. "Who are you talking to?"

The little boy looked up and saw his adoptive mother standing in the open doorway.

Oh, Jesus, it's Mom. Florence Sackler.

"Charlie," he answered out of little Cole's mouth.

"Charlie? Again?" his mother put a hand on her hip. "Honey, what's your imaginary friend saying to you this time?"

"His tyr-an-no-saurus will eat my bront-o-saurus!"

Cole looked back at Charlie, but he wasn't there. Cole was alone in his room.

"Oh, well, don't let him do that." She looked around the space. "I want you to pick up your room, Cole. It's a mess. I'll come back in a little while and it had better be done, okay?"

"Okay." Cole watched his mother as she left the room.

Cole looked back at Charlie, who was still sitting on the floor next to him with his dinosaur. The boy had a mischievous grin on his face.

"Your dinosaur gets eaten, and that's that!" Charlie said. He went, "Growl garr rowr!" as he manipulated his tyrannosaurus to attack the brontosaurus, pretending it was having dinner.

"No, Charlie, no!"

Cole wanted to punch his twin brother. It wasn't fair!...

... "Hey space man! Get your head out of the clouds!"

It was a new voice, an older kid, one of many.

Cole was suddenly on a playground during recess at school. Although he hadn't remembered the scenario in his bedroom with the dinosaurs, Cole knew exactly where he was and when this was happening. He was in third grade, the target of a handful of neighborhood bullies. It was the tableau from that photograph in the weird dark corridor he had been in after he'd died.

"Hey, space cadet! Com'ere!"

Cole was now looking out of his eight-year-old eyes at three of the bigger clowns in his class. He remembered that one of the henchmen was named Georgie. Bob Dooley was the ringleader.

"Don't be afraid, we want to talk to you!"

Cole tried to stop his legs from moving, but he was powerless to change his younger self's actions. He was witnessing them firsthand, but he couldn't do anything to influence a different outcome.

He *knew* that Georgie Whozit would do an end run around him, and then get on his hands and knees. Cole could even sense the kid was behind him, ready for the shove.

Bob came closer. "You know, Coley-Poley, you need to stop daydreaming so much. People might think you're *retarded* or something!"

Ha Ha Ha—laughs from the bullies and the gathering group of kids who wanted to watch.

"Leave me alone," Cole said weakly.

"What's that? I can't hear you, spaceman! Hey, you better pay attention. Something might *happen*—"

That's when the push came. Eight-year-old Cole tumbled backwards over Georgie.

Belly laughs all around.

Cole lay on the grass as the bullies walked away, slapping each other on the backs. None of the bystanders helped him up. They either laughed along with the assholes or they looked at him with pity.

One thing he remembered from that day—Cole decided to take self-defense lessons. Boxing or judo or something. He wasn't going to take it anymore...

... *Pow!* The fist inside the boxing glove smacked him on the left cheek.

Cole bounced on his feet a few steps as he assumed a defensive stance.

What the hell? What's happening to me?

Now he was in a boxing ring at the local gym, where he had taken lessons as a young teenager. The Latino kid he was matched against was good. Cole remembered that. It all came crashing back to him. He was, what, fourteen years old? He hadn't started the lessons until he was eleven. The kid opposing him looked to be about fourteen or fifteen. And he was moving in for an uppercut!

Cole blocked with his left and immediately executed a fast punch with his right, landing squarely on Jorge's nose. His adversary yelped and staggered back. He blinked and winced and, after a few seconds' delayed reaction, Jorge covered his face with both gloves, turned, and walked to the ropes. He forfeited the match.

A whistle blew. The coach approached Jorge to make sure he wasn't hurt too badly. Mr. Thorndyke turned his head to Cole and winked. "Good defense, Cole."

The teen nodded and climbed out of the ring. He grabbed the bottle of water that was waiting for him on the floor and swallowed several gulps before taking a towel and wrapping it around his neck.

How is this possible? I'm inside my fourteen-year-old body, performing his moves, but I can't say, "No, go over here *instead!" I have no control!*

As he walked to the dressing room for a shower, Cole recalled that day. Mr. Thorndyke would reclassify Cole and put him in an advanced class. The boxing lessons did him a world of good. It got Cole out of his shy shell and gave him more confidence. It didn't hurt in building his physique, either. He had always been tall and big-boned, but now what used to be indoor-introvert flabbiness was turning to muscle.

Cole remembered how angry he had been at that age, especially before starting the lessons. The bullies had made a regular habit out of picking on him, and one day he had a meltdown at school. After being shoved and pushed and teased for the umpteenth time, he simply started yelling like a mad person. One of the teachers on duty on the recess field came running and escorted Cole to the office. He was sent home, which was just as humiliating. From then on, he had become sullen and uncooperative at school. His grades dropped. He hated everyone and everything. Finally, his parents allowed him to take the boxing lessons he craved. He had channeled the anger into those leather, cushioned gloves.

The classes lasted until he was sixteen. Mr. Thorndyke left the gym and Mr. Landry took over. Cole didn't like Mr. Landry. From the get-go, Landry tended to belittle him in front of the others. It affected his boxing, so he quit when he became a junior in high school...

...*Slam!*

A gloveless bare-knuckled fist plowed into his face. Cole felt a heavier body fall back against a table, knocking over glasses and spilling liquid—it smelled like beer.

Now where was he?

"Get up, asshole!"

The man who'd hit him was prancing around, his fists raised.

Bob. Bob the bully.

Cole recalled the incident. He was eighteen and the year was 1966. He'd been drinking in a bar on the Lower East Side and Bob Dooley had come in. This time it was Cole who had initiated the fight. Already more than a little drunk, he had confronted Bob. "Remember me, you piece of shit?" Bob had been astounded that he'd run into Coley-Poley again, but he was also quite willing to make Cole take back the epithet.

The fight broke out in an instant. Bottles and glasses were broken, and tables were overturned. The few women in the place shrieked, while the men quickly picked sides and cheered on their chosen fighter. The bartender, meanwhile, called the police.

Cole got himself up off the table and ran at Bob. Even though he was drunk, his boxing experience paid off. He managed to get in some well-placed blows that knocked Bob off his feet. Blood spurted out of his nose. This made Bob more determined to whoop Cole's butt. He may not have had lessons, but he was a decent boxer. He got up quickly.

The brawl lasted another five minutes before approaching sirens could be heard. Bob backed Cole against the bar and bludgeoned him repeatedly with his fists. Cole, his right arm outstretched on the counter to keep himself from falling, felt a beer bottle at his fingertips. He stretched and grabbed hold of the neck—then swung it around with as much force as he could muster and broke it on Bob's head.

The fight ended.

Bob slumped to the floor, blood streaming out of the gash in his scalp.

Cole stumbled to a chair and sat down, put his face in his hands and...

… his surroundings changed again.

He felt cold air and the lighting was very bright. Cole removed his hands from his face and saw sterile white walls, an aluminum sink and toilet, and bars. He was sitting on a bunk, the mattress thin and smelly.

Oh, right. I had spent the night in jail with an A/C that was working overtime.

The cops had arrested him, got his cuts and scrapes treated at the emergency room, and promptly locked him in the slammer. Bob, on the other hand, had to get stitches and was treated for a concussion. Surprisingly, he didn't press charges.

Unfortunately, this was the beginning of repeat performances. Cole's anger needed management.

Cole opened his eyes and studied the water stain in the ceiling tiles above him. He was lying on a couch. Disoriented from all the scenery changes, Cole jerked up with a start…

…"Is something wrong, Cole?"

Dr. Patterson. The man was in his fifties and looked like the old actor Ralph Bellamy. What year was it now? Cole recalled going to a few sessions with Dr. Patterson not long after his third arrest, which was, what, six months or so after the first one? It was 1967 and Cole was nineteen. The most recent judge had ordered him to see a therapist, and Cole complied.

"Uh, no, sorry, I thought…never mind." Cole lay back down.

How do I get out of this time-jumping bullshit? Just get me back to Hotel Destiny, please!

"Shall we continue?" the doctor asked.

"Uh, sure."

"You had been telling me how your parents discouraged you from having an imaginary friend when you were a child."

"Oh. Right."

"You said you believed he was your twin brother?"

"Yeah. I mean, I knew I didn't have a twin brother. But I pretended I did."

"Why do you think you felt the need to invent a twin brother?"

"I don't know! I was five or six years old."

"But you just said a few minutes ago that you continue to talk to him when you're alone."

"I did?"

"Yes, Cole, you did. Something about 'Dream States'?"

He remembered that the Dream States had occasionally continued into his twenties, but after that they had become less frequent. Once he got into his thirties, they rarely happened at all, maybe one every two or three years. But back then? Yes, he was still "talking" to Charlie, his imaginary twin brother. There were times when Cole had thought he might be nuts.

Now he knew that he really *did* have a twin brother. What had become of him? He had heard the administrator at the orphanage say something about Charlie and his burn wounds. Why didn't the Sacklers ever *say something*? "Cole, you have a twin brother somewhere." Couldn't they have mentioned it? Wouldn't they have wanted to try and find Charlie? A brother is a brother!

It never happened. He had grown up believing Charlie was an imaginary friend, and yet, he had instinctively *known* that Charlie was real. Somehow, he was connected psychically to his brother, wherever he was.

"Cole?" the doctor asked. "I lost you there for a moment. Your mind doesn't seem to be on the session."

"Uh, sorry. Maybe I'm just not in the mood today."

Had he really said that at the time?

Cole closed his eyes again and felt the room shift. Through his eyelids he could tell that the lighting had changed. He opened his eyes and saw a very different ceiling. It was made of plaster rather than tile, and the paint was peeling.

He raised himself to view his surroundings. He was now lying on a double bed. Nightstands with lamps were on either side of him, but they were very old-fashioned. Drapes covered a window. A door led to what appeared to be a bathroom, and another one was shut with a chain-lock dangling down. The place was familiar.

Of course! It's one of the guest rooms in Hotel Destiny! He recognized the layout. Just the *feel* of the place was something he knew. The problem was that everything looked like it was from an era other than his own.

He got up and stood on his feet. A strange tingling went

down his back as he realized that he was most certainly in Room 308, where Bradley Granger had killed Theresa Flynn and then shot himself. Or, if he wanted to spin the scenario, it was where Cole, as a ghost, had struggled with Granger and *caused* the actor to shoot himself.

Cole heard music outside in the hallway. Or it was in one of the other rooms on the floor. A record player or radio was playing Fred Astaire singing, "Heaven, I'm in heaven...." What was that song? "Cheek to Cheek"—that was it.

He went to the bathroom, turned on the light, and looked in the mirror. Same bloodshot eyes. Same pale face and tired expression. Same tuxedo.

He was back in the hotel, that was for sure. But when?

Cole crossed the room to the door and opened it.

Down the hall, two gangster-types were standing outside Room 302, guarding the family suite. The music was coming from the apartment, and the door was open. Cole shut his own door behind him and walked in that direction.

At that moment, Curly Chadwick appeared from the room and spoke to one of the men. He then noticed Cole coming down the hall.

"Hello, sir," he said. "Is the music too loud? Are we disturbing you?"

"No," Cole answered. "Not at all."

"What room are you in?"

Cole gestured. "Down there. Three Oh Eight."

"Oh. I didn't realize that room was booked. I'm James Chadwick." He held out a hand.

Cole shook it. "Cole Sackler."

"Glad to meet you, Mr. Sackler. Would you like to come inside the apartment for a drink?" He winked and put a finger to his lips. "We thought we'd bring in the New Year right here in our suite before going downstairs to join the crowd. Why don't you join us for a quick one?"

14

Accompanied by Curly Chadwick, Cole stepped into the Apartment—Room 302—and followed the entry hall into the living room, where Miranda Flynn was standing, champagne glass in hand, talking to another gangster-type fellow. The room was populated by five other men and eight young women, the latter appearing to be party girls rather than wives. Two black servants stood at attention next to ice buckets containing bottles of bubbly. When one of them saw Cole, he immediately leaped into action, removed the bottle, grabbed a glass from a cart, poured the liquid into it, and handed it to Cole before the newcomer could say, "Happy New Year."

"Thank you," he said.

Just what New Year is this? When *am I*?

He figured he was sometime in the mid-1930s. Fred Astaire had just finished singing "Cheek to Cheek" on the radio, so it had to be after 1935, when that song had appeared in the movie *Top Hat*.

Chadwick said, "Excuse me a moment, I need to take care of something. Miranda, this is Mr. Sackler, he's staying down the hall." The big man then turned away and returned to talk to his men in the corridor.

Miranda was dressed in an elegant evening gown and looked spectacular, her blonde hair glistening, her blue eyes sparkling. She appeared to be in her early twenties.

Cole's birth mother.

She smiled and approached him. "Hello! Don't I know you from somewhere?"

He found himself tongue-tied now that he was aware of her relationship to him. Nothing could be more surreal than standing with her, drinking booze, and seeing his real mother in her vibrant, lovely youth.

"I'm, uh, I'm a guest at the hotel."

"I've seen you before, I think. Do you come here often?"

"Uh, yeah, I've been a guest a few times here. It's been a while, though. The last time I was here, I believe you and I met in the ballroom. You were alone, playing piano. I came in and we talked for a few minutes."

Miranda wrinkled her brow and cocked her head at him. "Really?"

"You talked about ghosts."

"Ghosts?" Then her eyes widened. "Oh! I *do* remember! Oh my, that was a long time ago. Five or six years, I think! You came in and…heavens, you were dressed exactly the same way, in a tuxedo. It's all coming back to me. I thought you looked very handsome and dashing!"

"I believe you were sixteen years old then," Cole said.

"Well, I'm twenty-one, now. Have I changed?"

Cole's voice caught and he had to clear his throat. "You've… you've grown into a beautiful young woman, and I'm honored to meet you again." He gave her a little bow.

Miranda laughed and said, "Thank you, my, aren't you a gentleman."

The thought suddenly crossed Cole's mind that Curly Chadwick might be his birth *father*. He and Chadwick were both tall, broad-shouldered men.

"If it's not too personal a question, are you, uh, are you and Curly, uh, Mr. Chadwick, an…item?"

Her finger jumped to her lips. "Shh!" She leaned in and whispered. "*No one* calls him 'Curly' except for me. He hates that name unless I'm the one says it. If he hears you call him that, you may not live to tell the tale!"

"Yikes, sorry. I'll be more careful."

She leaned in closer. "But everyone calls him Curly behind his back. He's going to go down in history as Curly Chadwick, not James Chadwick, whether he likes it or not!" She giggled.

Should I try warning her about the fire that will take place in this very apartment? Maybe not. She'll think I'm crazy. Besides, that's a decade or more away, I think. What year are we in now?

"How's the champagne?" Miranda asked.

Cole hadn't tasted it yet. He took a sip. "Very good!"

"It sure beats the awful stuff we had to drink during Prohibition, don't you think?"

Cole looked around the room. "Are these people all friends of yours?"

"They're Curly's friends. His 'associates,' as he calls them. I'm playing hostess, can't you tell? These girls, they're...they work at the hotel." Her chipper exterior shifted slightly as her eyes darted away. Cole could see that she didn't approve of the women...or the men.

"Wasn't the hotel closed for a while?" he asked.

She nodded. "We had to close in '31. My father—did you know him? Laurence Flynn?"

"Yes, I did."

"Then you know he was the owner and manager since he opened the place in 1917. Sadly, the big crash of '29 took a toll on him. He...he died in 1931 and I inherited the hotel. At the time, though, I couldn't make it work. I had to close the place. But Curly...Curly helped me get solvent again. We opened again in 1933, just in time for Prohibition to get repealed! That alone was a saving grace. Now we're doing very well."

"Are you...are you and Cur—Mr. Chadwick married?"

Miranda shook her head. "No. Curly wants to get hitched, but I'm...I'm not ready. Oh, speak of the devil!"

Chadwick appeared at their side. "My apologies. I had to tend to some business. How do you like my best girl, Mr. Sackler?"

"Uh, she's a charming hostess."

The big man wrapped a large arm around Miranda and squeezed her to him. She made a face that only Cole could see, and he then understood the situation. Curly Chadwick had bankrolled the re-opening of Hotel Destiny, and in exchange Miranda Flynn was obligated to be his girlfriend. She wasn't particularly happy about it, either.

"What business are you in, Mr. Sackler?" Chadwick asked after he let go of Miranda.

"Call me Cole. To tell the truth, I'm a hotel detective."

Chadwick raised his eyebrows. "Seriously? Where do you work?"

"New Jersey. I'm on vacation."

"What hotel in New Jersey? I have some associates in New Jersey."

Cole was stuck there. His eyes darted around the room and rested on the servant with the champagne bottle. "Uh, the Hotel Butler."

Chadwick frowned. "Where in New Jersey? What town?"

"Oh, it's downstate. You wouldn't know it."

"Try me."

Miranda interrupted. "Curly, when are you going to take me downstairs to dance? I want to join the party."

He looked at her. "Honey, we'll go down when I'm ready." Back to Cole. "Mr. Sackler, you look like someone who can handle himself well. I could maybe use a man with your hotel experience. How would you like to come to New York and work for us?"

"Here? At Hotel Destiny?"

"Yeah." Chadwick slapped Cole's left upper arm. "You served in the military, right?"

"Yes, I did."

"I can tell. I was in France, too. 26th Infantry. You?"

France? What's he talking about? Oh, right. World War I.

Cole had almost slipped and said he had served in Vietnam. "Believe it or not, I was in the 26th, too," Cole answered.

"Oh, yeah? Well, it was a big division. What regiment were you in? I was in the 102nd."

Uh oh. Can't do anything but take a stab at it. "Small world. I was in the 103rd."

"How about that. We were neighbors!" Chadwick slapped him on the shoulder again. "Did you kill any Germans?"

"I did." Eager to change the subject, Cole gestured with his free hand. "I love the way the hotel has been turned around. Are you the manager, now?"

"I am. Miranda's the owner, but I run the place, isn't that right, honey?" He squeezed her again, and she forced a smile.

Another gangster-type flanked by two heavies entered the room.

"Johnny! Happy New Year to you!" Chadwick said, moving to embrace the rough-looking character. He then brought the man over. "Miranda, this is Johnny Torrio, from Chicago. Johnny, this is Mr. Sackler. He's a hotel detective somewhere down in New Jersey."

Johnny Torrio? Cole vaguely recalled that he was a notorious mobster in the days of Al Capone. If Curly Chadwick was "associating" with the likes of him, then Chadwick was seriously up to no good.

The men shook hands and then Chadwick said, "Cole, my girl is dying to go downstairs and dance. I have to talk business with Johnny here. Would you mind escorting Miranda to the ballroom, maybe cutting a rug with her for a bit until I can break away?"

"I, uh, I'd be delighted."

"Thank you." He then pinched Cole's left cheek, harder than he needed to. "Just be a gentleman, all right?" It wasn't a request.

Cole wanted to punch the guy, but he kept his cool. "Certainly."

Rubbing his cheek, he turned to Miranda, who had an expression of disbelief on her face. Her jealous boyfriend was actually allowing her to dance with another man—and a stranger at that.

"Shall we?" Cole asked, extending a hooked arm.

Miranda took it and smiled. "Yes. We'll see you downstairs, Curly."

Chadwick waved them away and turned to Torrio. Cole led his *mother* out of the room and into the hallway.

"Shall we take the elevator or the stairs?" he asked.

"It's just one flight. Let's take the stairs."

Cole moved in that direction and stopped. Laurence and Theresa Flynn, dressed as they were at the Halloween party of 1917, stood in the way. They looked at him with disapproval.

"What's wrong?" Miranda asked. "Forget something?"

She can't see them.

"Remember when you told me that you see ghosts?" he asked.

"Yeah?"

"Do you see any now?"

"Nope."

Cole nodded. "Good." He escorted his mother past his grandparents and they both descended the stairs.

15

When they walked into the Grand Room, Cole was immediately struck by the difference in the décor to the previous Halloween parties he had attended in 1985 and 1917. This was a New Year's Eve party, so the ambiance was bright, festive, and colorful. A large banner strung above the stage proclaimed: HAPPY NEW YEAR 1936! There were no costumes this time, only stylish men's and women's evening wear. Nearly every man was in a tuxedo, so Cole fit right in, although the style of his 1985 tux was slightly off. ("It's a French tuxedo," he decided he would tell anyone who asked about it.) Everyone looked like they had stepped out of an Astaire/Rogers movie musical. The place was sparkling, due mostly to more lighting than what was in place in 1917. The huge chandelier was at full brightness, covering the couples on the dance floor with silver screen luminescence. Many-colored balloons were tied to furniture and placed on dining tables in lieu of flowers. Highboys also spotted the areas outside the dance floor, but there were also some comfy chair/sofa/coffee table combinations. Cole noted that Theresa Flynn's portrait had been re-hung next to her husband's. The band seemed to be interchangeable, however, with their counterparts in the other eras. This time, though, they played lavish pop songs and jazz numbers popular in the Depression years. They were currently in full swing with "Lullaby of Broadway."

"Come on, Cole," Miranda said, "let's dance." She led him to the middle of the floor, and they took positions. "You know how to dance, don't you?"

"Not really, but I've had lots of practice in the last twenty-four hours," he answered.

"What?"

"Never mind."

They began to move in the ballroom swing fashion that was just becoming *de rigueur* in that period.

I'm dancing with my birth mother. This is blowing my mind.

It struck him that he was suddenly enjoying himself. He hadn't felt this good in *ages*. Considering that he'd literally been hopping *through* ages, Cole found that thought ironic.

"Oh, look, do you see that couple over by the bar?" Miranda asked.

He gazed over and saw an attractive young woman in a flashy dress and wearing a big feather cap in her brown hair. She had a drink in hand and was talking to a professorial-looking man with bookworm eyeglasses.

"What about them?"

"That's Ethel Merman and Clifford Odets. She's a big Broadway star. You've probably heard her songs from *Anything Goes*? 'You're the Top' and 'I Get a Kick Out of You'?"

"I know who she is. She's famous for 'Everything's Coming Up Roses.'"

Miranda frowned. "I don't know that one. What's it from?"

Oops. "I don't know. I think I'm getting her mixed up with someone else."

"And he's the hot new playwright on Broadway. Did you see *Awake and Sing*?"

"No. I'm not much of theater guy."

The band segued into a slower number, "When I Grow Too Old to Dream," that necessitated Cole and his mother to dance closer together, cheek to cheek. The song lyrics, combined with the situation, were doubly paradoxical.

"You're a nice man, Cole Sackler," Miranda said in his ear. Her inflection made him uncomfortable. This was *mother*, for Christ's sake! Besides, Curly Chadwick would probably not take it lightly if his girl might be coming on to another man.

He was about to make an excuse to get another drink and break off the dance, when Cole saw, over Miranda's shoulder, the man in the black cloak and white mask standing at the wall beneath the Flynns' portraits. He stuck out like a sore thumb, the only one wearing such a getup, yet no one else noticed him.

The man was staring at Cole.

He's my twin brother. Charlie. I know it. He must be.

Miranda noticed his audible gasp. "What's wrong?"

"Pardon me, Miranda. My brother's here. I'll be right back." He broke away and skirted through the dancing couples until he left the dance floor. The man in the mask moved quickly, heading toward the ballroom doors. More people got in Cole's way as he blurted, "Excuse me, excuse me!" In his haste he ran into a servant carrying a tray of drinks. The man spilled the contents, which crashed to the carpet. "I'm so sorry! Pardon me!" Cole kept rushing until he reached the doors and flew into the foyer.

The guy was gone.

Did he go up the stairs? Down the stairs? Into the elevator?— the gold doors were just closing. Into the access hallway to the kitchen?

Cole trotted to the Grand Stairs and went down halfway. He was all alone. He got far enough to duck his head and peer into the ground floor lobby, but he didn't see the man.

His heart hammering in his chest, Cole turned around and hustled up the stairs past the second-floor landing to the third. Again, there was no one to be seen.

"Damn it."

Admitting defeat, Cole returned to the foyer and re-entered the ballroom. He scanned the dance floor to see if Miranda was still there, but of course she wouldn't be because he'd abandoned her. Instead, she was standing at the bar and ordering a drink. He went over to her.

"Sorry, Miranda, I thought I saw him, but he got away."

She didn't look at him.

"Hello?" He waved a hand. "I apologize, it was rude of me to just leave you there."

She didn't acknowledge his words or gestures.

Oh, hell, I'm invisible again.

"Hey, everyone!" he shouted, testing that theory.

No one turned their heads to him.

How in blazes did this invisible/visible thing work? It was driving him mad!

"Wait a minute," he said aloud. "Could it be...?"

Cole turned and left the ballroom again. Since there were a few people in the foyer, he headed for the Employees Only door that accessed the kitchen. He went through it, stood alone for a moment, and concentrated on *being seen*. Then he retraced his steps, went back into the Grand Room, and found Miranda still at the bar.

"Hi," he said.

She turned to him and smiled. "Did you find your brother?"

It worked!

That was the trick. He could toggle the visibility only when *no one was looking* and by concentrating on the goal. He had to be alone, or at least not in anyone's line of sight for the transformation to succeed.

Why couldn't have Agnieszka just told him that? Sheesh.

And, speaking of the gypsy fortune teller, there she was, sitting at her card table over by the Flynns' portraits. She hadn't been there earlier, but she was present now.

"Are you all right for a bit, Miranda?" he asked. "I need to speak to someone I know. Can I catch up with you later?"

"Sure. Here comes Curly anyway."

Cole turned to the doorway and saw the big man and his goons entering, shaking hands, and greeting guests.

"Thank you for dancing with me," she said. "And you're a fine dancer. Much better than Curly, anyway."

"Thanks." Cole took her hand and kissed it. "It means a lot to have been able to dance with you. More than you'll ever know."

With that, he left his bewildered mother and crossed the ballroom floor to Agnieszka's table. FREE PALM READINGS.

"Hello, Agnieszka."

The woman smiled knowingly and fluttered her long eyelashes for a mini-second. "Happy Near Year, Mr. Sackler. Have you discovered your destiny yet?"

16

"Miranda Flynn is my mother, isn't she." It wasn't a question.

"Hm." Agnieszka interlocked her fingers beneath her chin and rested her head on them, her elbows on the table. "You catch on quick."

He nodded at Curly Chadwick, who was across the room still doing the glad-hand. "And what about him? Is that gangster my real father?"

"That is indeed a question."

"Oh, for God's sake, what kind of an answer is that? What does that mean? Stop talking in riddles. Why can't you just tell me things?"

"There are rules."

"Who makes them?"

"I don't know."

"Who enforces them?"

"Mr. Sackler, you are asking the wrong questions. You need to be continuing your journey. If you want answers, you must look for them."

"What about the fire? Did I get my burns in the 1948 fire that consumed Room 302?"

Her eyes playfully went up to ceiling as if she knew the answer but simply didn't want to tell him.

Cole cursed, threw up his hands, and then crossed his arms. The whole thing was frustrating. He turned to watch the dancers as the band shifted into playing "It Ain't Necessarily So," as if that was the answer to his earlier question. He could see Chadwick with his arm around Miranda as they spoke to other couples at a furniture arrangement near the bar.

He swiveled back to Agnieszka. "I keep seeing the man with the black cloak and white mask. He must be a ghost, too. I've seen him in different years, different eras. I'm thinking that he's my twin brother, Charlie. Am I right?"

She shrugged. "Under the mask, he is a mirror image of you."

"I take it that's a yes. I need to talk to him."

"When you finally come face to face with him, then you'll have all the answers you seek."

"Is he the serial killer? Did he kill *you?*"

"Cole, who are you talking to?"

Miranda's voice startled him. Cole whirled around to find her standing with a martini in each hand.

"Oh, hi, is that for me?" he asked.

"Yeah, here, I brought you a drink. I saw you over here talking to the wall."

"No, I was talking to—" He turned to introduce her to Agnieszka, but of course the fortune teller and her table were gone. "I was talking to the portraits of your parents." He indicated the paintings. "Your mother was a beautiful woman."

"Here, take the damn drink, will you?" He did so and had a sip. It was strong and cold, just how he liked it. "Yes, she was beautiful, and she was trouble. I didn't inherit her looks, but her trouble was passed down to me."

"That's not true," Cole said. "You're the loveliest woman in the room."

He was feeling awkward and uncomfortable again. In fact, he was downright queasy. Miranda Flynn was his mother, and he was talking to her as if she might be a prospective conquest. He had to get out of there.

"Listen, Miranda, to tell you the truth, I'm not feeling so good. I think I need to splash water in my face or something. Will you excuse me?"

"Sure. It figures you'd keep your distance when Curly's in the room. All the men do. Would it make any difference to you if I said I'd like to keep my distance from Curly, too?"

Over her shoulder, Cole saw Chadwick conversing with men who looked like bankers, but the gangster's eye was on him. The man was watching how Cole behaved with his girl.

Now he really did feel nauseated. Carrying the martini, Cole gave a little bow to Miranda and said, "Excuse me, please. I'm sorry, I need to...." He then left her again and headed for the doors.

"I enjoyed it while it lasted," she called out to him, but not too loudly.

Cole made it to the foyer and headed for the men's washroom. The last time he'd been in there, he was chasing after Charlie. He'd stepped into a portal, or whatever it was, when he'd opened the supply closet. It hadn't been pleasant, so he was determined to avoid that little trap.

He set the barely drunk martini on the counter, went to a stall, closed the door, dropped to his knees, and promptly threw up into the toilet.

After the heaving was done, he sat there on the floor, trying to catch his breath.

So, who ever said a ghost couldn't vomit? Here, have some ectoplasm, ha ha!

Then he passed out...

... No, he was just resting—or so he thought when his eyes opened—in the seventh-floor stairwell. He knew where he was from the fading number seven that was painted on the brick wall by the metal door leading to the hallway and rooms. It was the stairwell for the fire escape, at the far end of the corridor from the elevators.

The truth was that he *had* passed out, right there on the stairs. He had an empty bottle of Jack Daniel's in his hand, and he felt the weight of his Smith & Wesson revolver in his pocket.

What the hell?

This all seemed familiar.

He managed to stand by holding on to the railing. Then he noticed he wasn't wearing the tuxedo. He was dressed in "night manager" clothing—basically a thrift store suit. It had been his go-to look back in the day.

Cole moved to the door. He opened it, went through, and he was on the seventh floor. The scuzzy condition of the hallway, the loud disco music coming from an open door and the raucous hard rock emanating from another indicated to him that he was in the 1970s. In fact, the scene came rushing back at him.

This is one of those memory things Agnieszka told me about. The clothing is a clue. I'm re-living this. I'm not really here. Right?

It was around one in the morning. The only people on the floor were junkies, dealers, hookers, and johns. The year was 1976, to be precise, and Cole Sackler, in his role as night manager and hotel detective, was about to discover his first murder victim in the building.

He recalled that he had been making the rounds on the twelve floors and using the fire escape stairwell to access each one. He always carried his pistol in those days because one never knew what one might encounter in sleazebag central. He had walked down from the eighth floor, when something or someone had hit him on the head. He had lost consciousness.

Or had it been a sudden Dream State?

Cole didn't know. He had been aware only of coming to on the cold concrete floor with an empty bottle of Jack in his hand.

Now it was replaying.

A sense of dread enveloped his chest as he moved toward the open door. 711. He knew what he would find inside.

Hutch Butler had been a two-bit drug dealer and pimp. His office was 42nd Street and his territory was Times Square and its environs. He'd been using Hotel Destiny as a sanctuary of sorts, where he would shack up with one of his girls or maybe sleep off a binge that lasted a few days. The man had been thirty-four when he died, but this was a guy who was as tough as nails. He and Cole had an understanding. Cole got a kickback from Hutch, and in return, Cole left him alone.

Hey, it was Times Square in the '70s.

On this particular night, though, someone had shot Hutch Butler in the head. The man was found sitting at the only table in the guest room, face down, blood and brains dripping onto the floor. Whoever had killed him had left the door open and the music blaring.

It was an awful sight, but Cole had seen worse in Vietnam. He was more put out by the prospect of calling and having to deal with the cops.

"You live by the street, you die by the street," Sergeant Redenius said.

The policeman was suddenly standing next to him while the forensics team worked the scene of the crime. A photographer took shots of the victim from several angles.

It was another one of those jump cuts that occurred in the memory pockets. *Time will play games with you,* Agnieszka had said.

"This place is a pig sty, Mr. Sackler," Redenius said. "Fingerprints will be useless. This guy has probably had every streetwalker and every junkie in the precinct up here in the room. There are hundreds of different prints. You have any idea who was here in the room with him tonight?"

"No," Cole said. "To tell you the truth, Hutch usually kept to himself when he was in the hotel. I never had any trouble from him."

Redenius glanced down at Cole's feet. "You have blood on your shoes."

"Yeah, I know. I stepped in it when I found him."

"Well, let's keep people out of here for now, okay?"

Cole nodded, left New York's Finest to their jobs, and went to the elevator. It came quickly, he got in, and rode it alone down to the second floor. When it opened, he scanned the dark foyer. No one was there. The New York Street Skunk were all up in their rooms.

But there was a light on in the men's washroom on the other side of the foyer.

Now what…?

Maybe the janitor had left it on.

Cole walked across and entered…and the place was eerily empty and clean. No used hypodermics were in sight, no shit on the walls, no piss on the floor.

Just a little while ago I threw up in the stall, back on December 31, 1935. New Year's Eve. Weird.

He went into the stall, inspected it, and came out…

… The light shifted. He felt a light tremor in the floor.

Music wafted in from the foyer. Someone was singing "The Talk of the Town."

Cole walked out to see men and women in evening dress.

He was back at the New Year's Eve party and dressed in his ghostly tuxedo.

A man came toward him, heading for the washroom, and nearly bumped into him.

"Hey, watch it!" Cole blurted.

The man didn't notice him.

Ah.

Cole said hello to a woman who was making a beeline to the ladies' room. She didn't acknowledge him.

I'm invisible again. I was alone in the elevator and in the bathroom. The "trick" works even when I don't concentrate on it. Being by myself with no looking does it. Fine with me.

Not wanting to go into the ballroom and face his mother again, Cole decided to go downstairs to the privacy of his old office. He wasn't sure if anyone occupied it on that date in history, but he'd take the chance. He moved across the foyer back to the lifts. He pressed the button to call one of the cars, and he overheard one of Curly Chadwick's henchmen—the man called "Shake"—talking to a party guest a few feet away. Cole had seen the gangster in Room 302 earlier, when they were all having drinks in the apartment before heading downstairs. The guest was surreptitiously handing over a wad of bills to Shake, who said, "Take the elevator to the fifth floor. Knock on the door to Room 510. Madeline will answer it. You tell her Shake sent you. You'll then get your pick of the ladies and she'll take it from there."

"Thanks," the man said. "Just the way to start the new year, eh? Then I'll join you for the poker game at two o'clock. Oh, and I want to place a bet on the horse race."

"Room 1107 for poker. You already bought in, right?"

"Sure!"

"The other high stakes games are in 1108, 1109, and 1110."

"Poker's my game."

"Okay, see you then. Now go have a good time."

The elevator arrived and the man got in. Cole decided to wait for the other one.

So, it was clear. Curly Chadwick was using the hotel for illegal activities. Gambling, prostitution, and who knew what else.

The elevator doors opened, and Cole stepped inside. He was alone again.

As soon as the doors closed, the bottom of the car dropped and Cole fell, flailing and screaming, into empty darkness once again.

17

The terrifying sensation of somersaulting through a void was akin to what Cole thought a heart attack might feel like. It went on and on...until it was just as abruptly all over.

He found himself sitting in a wooden chair at a polished wood table. The lights were bright. The American flag, limp on a stand, was a few feet in front of him against the wall. He could see the head and shoulders of a man wearing a black robe, positioned higher to the right and behind a podium-like structure. Another man in a police officer's uniform stood nearby.

I'm in a courtroom.

Indeed, Cole looked around him and shivered from the memory. The year was 1968. Norma, a woman he'd been seeing, called the cops on him one night when he had been drunk and, apparently, abusive. He had no recollection of it, but the eyewitnesses and the bruises she bore around her neck proved it had happened. It had been a dark period for Cole. Looking back at those years after high school when he was aimless, unhappy, and drinking heavily, he was simply and frighteningly another person. The anger issue was a serious problem. He'd been arrested for public brawling a few times. He'd had to pay fines and even stay a few nights in jail. But this crime...it all came to a head with this one.

Norma Breem worked at a diner at the corner of Eighth Avenue and 39th Street. She was around his age, and she was street-smart, tough, and gorgeous. She liked to drink, too, but after three months, seven dates, and two unpleasant experiences when his Mean Drunk emerged, she had called off the relationship, such as it was.

Cole, feeling down and sorry for himself, partook of a bottle of Irish whiskey and went to the diner while Norma was waitressing. He confronted her, she told him to get lost, and he attacked her. The original charge was attempted murder, but his public defender miraculously managed to get it reduced to assault in exchange for a guilty plea.

He was ashamed.

"Mr. Sackler, before I pronounce sentence," the judge said, "do you have anything to say to the Court?"

Cole remembered the nervousness he had felt that day as he cleared his throat and answered, "Yes, sir."

"Please stand."

He did so and spoke as honestly as he could.

"Your Honor, I acknowledge that I have a drinking problem. The incident for which I've been convicted occurred when I was out of my head. I don't even remember it, as I've stated in my sworn affidavit. But that's no excuse. Dr. Patterson has submitted a letter detailing my history of what he calls blackouts. This was one of those times, Your Honor. I'm truly sorry for what I did to Miss Breem. I will endeavor to stop drinking and be a better person. Thank you."

With that he sat down.

"Thank you for that, Mr. Sackler. I'm going to hold you to it. You're to spend five months in the New York City Department of Corrections facility at Rikers Island, with probation for two years after sentence is served."

The judge banged the gavel and that was it. Cole didn't look at Norma Breem, who was sitting in the courtroom behind him to the right.

Court was adjourned, and the bailiff escorted the prisoner out...

...into sunlight in the general population yard at Rikers.

Another time hop.

Cole was dressed in the standard prison jumpsuit. He was allowed up to two hours a day outside in good weather and he always took advantage of it. It was a rough and dangerous place to be, but he had already spent a lot of time in the Times Square neighborhoods of New York City. He was a big guy, he knew how to fight, and he exuded a cantankerous, don't-mess-with-me attitude that other inmates innately respected.

For most of his stay at Rikers, he had been a loner. He didn't join any gangs, he didn't make any friends, and he did what he was told.

As Cole strolled toward the bleachers, where he usually sat for a spell after walking around the track by himself, he couldn't recall any specific day in prison that stood out from others. He was aware he was re-living one of those days, but he didn't have a clue when it might be or why it was replaying.

He climbed the bleachers to the next-to-highest bench and sat. Cole watched the other prisoners stake out their territories in an unspoken rivalry between separate gangs of men who had found in each other similar views and prejudices. Violence often broke out. The prison hospital was always operating at full capacity. Cole hadn't witnessed any deaths, but there were some close calls.

"Animals," a voice next to him proclaimed. "All animals."

Cole turned to see the man in the black cloak and white mask sitting a few feet away from him on the same bench. He turned his head and stared at Cole through the holes in the mask.

What the hell is he doing here? I don't believe this.

Cole decided to run with it. "Where have you been, Charlie?" he asked. "I've been looking for you."

The other man was silent for a moment, and then he responded. "I've always been within arm's reach."

Cole nodded. Somehow that made sense to him.

"We need to get together when I'm out. I miss you. We haven't talked in a long time. And why are you wearing that costume here?"

Charlie said, "What you need to do when you get paroled—and you will get paroled for good behavior—congratulations for that—what you should do is join the army."

"The army?"

"It will help you become disciplined, it will help you with your anger problem, and you won't get to drink as much. It will be a positive experience"

"Wouldn't I have to go to Vietnam?"

"They even take ex-cons as long as it's just a misdemeanor charge."

"Hey, whitey!" came a voice some feet away, down below on the ground.

Cole turned away from his twin and focused on one of his fellow inmates. He was a member of the gang of African Americans, someone who wasn't his friend per se, but a guy who acknowledged him with a nod every now and then.

"What do you want?" Cole hollered.

"You're talking to yourself. You know you do that a lot?"

"All the time. I'm my best friend."

The prisoner laughed, waved, and moved on.

Cole turned back to his brother, but of course he wasn't there.

The horn blew and the usual guard announced over the PA that "recess" was over. "Time to come in from the playground. Hope nobody got hurt on the monkey bars."

Ha. Ha. You think you're funny, Officer Thompson.

Cole would like to punch Officer Thompson, but that would be acting on his anger. The prison shrink wouldn't approve. Cole had agreed to spend time with the quack while he was serving his sentence. That was one of the reasons he got out after doing three and a half months instead of the full five.

He climbed down the bleachers, walked across the yard, ignored the rabble around him, and went through the door into...

...the hotel elevator. The one he'd entered at the 1936 New Year's Eve party after feeling sick in the washroom.

The golden doors closed. He was alone in the car.

What was all that about? Did that really happen back at Rikers? Is that how I decided to join the army? Did I talk to Charlie then?

He remembered that when he had entered the elevator earlier, he was on his way down to the first floor to hide in his office. And yet the lift was now going *up*.

Cole was too tired to care. All this jumping in and out of time periods and re-living unpleasant memories was exhausting. Would it ever end? Was this going to be his entire existence for the rest of infinity?

Maybe this really was hell. After he'd died—no, been *murdered*—he had landed in the hot spot.

The elevator stopped at floor ten. The doors opened, revealing another hallway in disrepair, a mirror image of all the other floors. His senses told him it was morning, sometime before noon.

He instinctively knew he wasn't on the cusp of 1936 anymore. This was how he remembered the floor looking during his employment at the hotel.

Tenth floor. Of course. There was only one reason why he was here now.

He was going to find another body in one of the rooms.

Oh, yeah. I remember this one, all right. How could I forget?

18

All his senses were stimulated as Cole walked down the tenth-floor hallway. He smelled the medley of marijuana smoke, garbage, and piss. Some lighting fixtures worked while others didn't, which added to the already trashy appearance. He heard music—this time Fleetwood Mac's "Dreams"—coming from one of the rooms, no doubt playing on a portable radio. God knew he didn't want to *touch* anything—there was no telling what he might catch. The taste in his mouth was his own bile, for his stomach was already preparing for what he was about to see.

The year was 1978. Sex, drugs, rock and roll, and more drugs. It was the nature of the beast in those days, especially at Hotel Destiny, a stone's throw from the pit that was Times Square.

The building was full of New York Street Skunk.

He passed a room with its door open. 1002. Inside was a black pimp and two of his white women, shooting up in plain sight. Cole stopped, said, "You might want to close this," and proceeded to shut their door.

Moving on, he encountered even more rooms with doors wide open. 1005 and 1007—the occupants were having a party and didn't care who saw the cocaine and needles.

At the end of the hallway was Room 1015, right near the fire escape stairwell. The door was closed, but Cole knew that she was inside. He knocked.

"Cindy? You awake?"

He knocked again and used his master key to unlock the door and open it.

The twenty-nine-year-old blonde woman was on the bed,

alive, but in a stupor. Thin, petite, and pretty when she wasn't stoned. The elastic band she'd used to tie off her arm was loose and lying by her side, as was the used hypo. Her eyes fluttered as he came in and she half-smiled.

"Colllllle," she purred. "Back...for more?"

"Aw, Cindy," he said. "You said you weren't going to do that again."

Cindy Walker was not a prostitute. In fact, she was a nurse who until recently worked at Roosevelt Hospital uptown. She had somehow become addicted to heroin, lost her job, spent her savings on dope, was evicted, and became homeless. Cole had met her before she would have had to fall into a trap of having to sell her body and soul, and he brought her to the hotel instead. For seven weeks, things were pretty good. They had something called a relationship. She tried hard to stop using and went days without doing so, but three times Cole had checked in on her to find that she'd had a fix.

"You're killing yourself!" he growled at her. "I can't have you here if you keep doing this!"

Slurring her words and speaking slowly, Cindy told him to go away. "You don't love me. I'm just...meat to you."

"That's not true!"

She narrowed her glassy eyes at him and said, "You like booze. What's...the difference?"

"I can quit drinking."

"Bull...shit. You can't admit...you're an...alcoholic."

It made Cole angry to hear those words. "Cindy, you have to get out. You have until morning to get your shit together and leave the hotel. I'm sorry. It's over between us. I gave you a chance and you blew it."

"No," she said. "I didn't blow it...you did."

Cole couldn't control himself. The rage quickly built inside him and he needed a release. The closest thing within reach was a lamp. He grabbed it and threw it against the wall, shattering the already burnt bulb inside. He stormed out of the room, leaving the door open. He made for the stairwell, opened the door, and went inside...

... The lighting shifted. The floor trembled.

Before he could go down the stairs, he heard voices in the hallway on the other side of the door. Cole paused as he recognized the familiar tone of Sergeant Redenius of the NYPD.

Another time jump, I guess.

Cole opened the stairwell door to see, once again, a group of policemen milling outside Room 1015.

Redenius was speaking to another cop, who was writing on a pad. "The hotel detective—Coleman Sackler—says he got a call from Room 1013 reporting a gunshot. He came up here and found her on the bed like that. He said her name is Cindy Walker, but we'll have to check the ID, make sure that's her real name. Sackler admitted she was unregistered. Probably a street person who got a room for the privacy of shooting up. Sounds like he was getting a little on the side in exchange. He was downstairs when she was killed. No one saw anything. There are no suspects."

"Isn't this just like what happened to that drug dealer a couple of years ago? What was his name?"

Cole answered, "Hutch Butler," but neither man heard him. They continued talking as if he weren't there.

"Hutch Butler," Redenius said. "Shot in the head just like Ms. Walker here, if that's her name. And just like Agnieszka Preisner, back in '72."

"Hey!" Cole called, waving his arms. He was only a few feet away from them. "I'm standing right here!"

They ignored him. Cole was an invisible ghost again, unseen, unheard, unimportant.

The other cop frowned. "There was another murder before I joined the force?"

"Yeah, 1972. She was a maid here at the hotel. Someone shot her in the basement, in the boiler room. Same M.O. The round went through her skull and was embedded in the wall. It was a match to what we found in the Butler case. We're pretty sure the same perp killed them both—at least we know it was the same gun, anyway. How much do you want to bet that we're dealing with the same killer here tonight?"

"Where's Sackler now?"

"Downstairs in his office. The guy's a drunk. He seems to be taking this one pretty hard. It's the second murder in the hotel on his watch. The maid—that was before he started working here."

Cole moved closer to the open door of 1015. He was aware of what he would see, but he had to do it anyway.

Cindy Walker was half-on, half-off the bed, her clothing torn, her head a mess of blood and bone fragments. Truly horrible. It was a ghastly sight, made even more repulsive because Cole had been intimate with her for a short while. His fingerprints were probably all over the room and her things. Would the police consider him a suspect?

He stepped into the room, not because he wanted a closer look. It was to say, "I'm sorry, Cindy. I shouldn't have gotten mad and left you."

Cole turned to leave, and his point of view crossed the open door to the bathroom. In the mirror over the sink, he clearly saw the man in the black cloak and white mask standing behind him.

Cole whirled around to confront the phantom, but of course, he wasn't there.

Charlie did this. Charlie's the killer.

Cole went back into the hallway, where the police were still talking.

"Why does the perp have a thing for shooting people in the head?" the cop asked.

"Who knows," Redenius answered. "He's like that Son of Sam guy. Freaks. They're all freaks. Come on, we need to get the scene processed. The smell is getting to me."

The odor was getting to Cole, too. Why was he being reminded of all these horrible events in his past? What did they have to do with his "heritage," as Agnieszka called it?

He entered the stairwell and took the steps two at a time all the way down to the ground floor. The bottom exit was near the reception desk, which was currently manned by Crystal. She had been an employee at the time of Cindy's murder. The last time he had seen and spoken to Crystal they had talked about drug dealer Byron Chavez. If Cole remembered correctly, Chavez was indeed in residence at Hotel Destiny on the seventh floor when Cindy was murdered. Perhaps *he* was the killer? It made sense. He might have also shot Hutch Butler, who was a business rival. As for Agnieszka, the maid, who knew? Chavez could have been hanging around the hotel before Cole was hired.

He couldn't recall if his 1978 self had suggested that possibility to Redenius.

Cole went to his office and shut the door. First things first—grab the bottle of whiskey from the drawer and take a few healthy swigs. Then, sitting in the chair behind his desk, he tried to get his head around everything that was happening. He had learned a lot about himself since he had "died." His dreams and fantasies about having a twin brother named Charlie had turned out to be true. He'd found out who his birth mother was—Miranda Flynn—and that his grandfather Laurence had built Hotel Destiny. There was also a good possibility that Cole had received his burn scars from the 1948 fire that had broken out in Room 302. Was *that* a memory he was destined to relive during this hellacious journey through his past? Whatever—it was strangely ironic that years later he would be employed as the night manager and hotel detective in the building that his grandfather had opened. Cole was intrinsically linked to this haunted place. In many ways, it was always his *home.*

RRRRRRRIIIIINGGGG!

The goddamned phone always startled him when it rang. Cole picked up the receiver and answered, "Sackler," out of habit.

"Sackler? J. T. here."

Oh, great. The boss before Marvin Trent.

J. T. Dunlap was a controversial real estate developer in New York who had made a living buying foreclosed buildings and turning them into profitable dumps. He had bought Hotel Destiny from the estate of Miranda Flynn in 1951 after the building had sat derelict for three years following her death in the 1948 fire. Dunlap repaired most of the damage on the third floor—although the rooms remained unuseable—and re-opened the hotel as a transient, flophouse joint that was perfect and just in time for the decline of the Times Square area and theatre district. Dunlap knew he could run the hotel cheaply, attract low-paying customers, and turn a profit. Dunlap hired Cole in 1974 to be the night manager and hotel detective.

"Hi, J. T. What's up?"

"Are the police still there?"

"I just came from the tenth floor, sir. They're still here."

"Jesus. Another murder. This won't be good, Sackler. Where the hell were you? You're supposed to be the goddamned security!"

"Sir, I was downstairs trying to keep the riff raff *out* of the building, like I always do. I can't be in every single room on all twelve floors at the same time. How was I supposed to know the woman would get shot?"

"I know, I know. Still…the killer got in somehow. Are we going to be liable in any way? I've already alerted my attorney."

"I don't think so, sir. It's not our fault. We're two blocks from Times Square. You know what a cesspool that area is. Shit happens. I wish we could catch the bastard, though."

"I do, too. All right, Sackler, keep me informed. And for God's sake, keep an eye out. We can't let this happen again."

Cole hung up the phone and reached for the Jack Daniel's again. After pouring a serious amount into an empty glass that happened to be on his desk, he leaned back in his chair and closed his eyes.

Charlie.

Was it possible that Charlie held a kind of grudge against him? Cole had been adopted by loving parents. What about Charlie?

More memories returned. After Cole had been released from Rikers in late 1968 and prior to joining the army, he had spent a little time indulging his fantasy that he had a twin brother.

Cole had gone searching for him in the real world.

19

As Cole sat in his office in Hotel Destiny, he allowed his mind to enter one of his beloved Dream States.

The dark time didn't end with Cole's brief prison sentence. It was true that he was released in three and a half months for good behavior, as he was a model inmate. He avoided fights, kept to himself, often went to the prison library, and never looked others in the eyes. He'd been warned about that. Sometimes just meeting another man's gaze got one into trouble.

His parents, the adoptive ones he'd grown up with, were still alive in 1968. The Sacklers still loved him, but something had changed in their relationship with him after he left high school. They strongly disapproved of his drinking and getting into hot water with the law. Fred Sackler had bailed Cole out of jail one too many times. After his release, Cole went to live with them again, saying it was on a temporary basis. He'd told them of his plans to join the army. His father heartily approved. His mother went along with it, probably agreeing that the discipline would do Cole some good.

Cole enlisted at a recruiting center in Manhattan in January 1969. He had nearly a month before he had to go to basic training, so living at home again wasn't too problematic. There was some tension at times. One night he came home drunk and his father made him leave. Cole slept in Washington Square Park and almost got into a scuffle with some college boys, but he kept his cool.

During this period, Cole "talked" to Charlie more than he had done since he was child. He was careful not to do it at home. His mother and father already thought there was something wrong with him. Cole didn't want to upset them. He did, though, ask them from what agency he had been adopted. It was a place in Queens called Green Garden.

One cold, January at nearly midnight, Cole took the subway to Queens and found the building in question. The place was still in operation then, although it closed not long after, sometime in the early '70s. He didn't know why that happened. Probably financial problems—that was usually the case.

As Green Garden was still in business, there were children in residence. That meant staff were working inside as well. The administrative offices, however, would be closed. The trick would be to get to their files without anyone seeing him. The way he did it was risky.

Cole went around to the back of the building to find a small employee parking lot and a trash dumpster. A rear door most likely went to the kitchen. It made sense. In his experience, food garbage usually had to be thrown out, and there was always easy access to do so. He also figured that a janitor would most likely do clean-up work at night, when the kids were asleep. Cole gambled on his timing being right.

He was in luck. It wasn't long before a man came out of the door to empty three bags of garbage into the dumpster. Cole flattened himself against the back wall, unseen in the shadows. When the employee was in front of the dumpster, hauling the bags one at a time into it, his sightline didn't include the rear door. Cole moved quickly, slipped inside, and indeed found himself in an alcove next to the kitchen. No one else was around. He moved swiftly through swinging double doors into the dining room. There were highchairs and small tables, as well as a couple of big ones for adults. The janitor had left a mop and bucket in the middle of the floor, where he had been working.

Cole continued his infiltration by leaving the dining room and following a hallway. One direction was well-lit and seemed to lead where Cole sensed more staff and the sleeping children would be present. The other way was dark. No need to keep the lights on in that section of the agency. That's the way Cole went.

He hit pay dirt after rounding a few corners. Cole passed three offices with name plaques on the doors, and then he came to a room marked RECORDS. Of course, the door was locked.

Cole looked both ways down the hall just in case some lone staff member might be patrolling the joint. He then pulled from his pocket a set of thin metal picks. It was something he'd learned about at Rikers. Lockpicks were like gold in the prison black market. Some of the more adventurous inmates used them to get into food storage, medical supplies, and other prohibited areas. While Cole never did that sort of thing, he once obtained a set of the tools and spent some time learning how to use them.

It took six minutes for him to successfully pick his way inside. The door closed behind him, and he removed a small flashlight from his pocket. It wouldn't do to turn on the overhead lights. He moved the beam around the room, which contained nothing but filing cabinets, a table, and chairs. A – Z.

First, he went to the S drawer, opened it, and quickly found a file folder marked SACKLER. He took it to the table, sat, aimed the flashlight on the pages, and went through it.

The infant, "Coleman," no last name, had come to them through a state-run organization in the fall of 1948. The birth mother and father were unknown. Coleman's date of birth was estimated to be June or July of that year. He had been a ward of the state for three months prior to coming to the orphanage.

There was no mention of a twin brother.

Burn wounds were noted, and there was a report from a plastic surgeon who had done the work. The baby had received burns on his left leg, hip, and side. Skin grafting was performed, and the lesions were still healing when the boy arrived at the agency.

There were several notations of potential adoptions, but when the parents saw the burned skin, they asked to see another child. The Sacklers, however, didn't mind. Fred and Florence adopted little Coleman in December of '48.

He'd grown up thinking his birthday was July 4— Independence Day, which was what he and his parents always celebrated as such. After reading the file, Cole knew that this likely wasn't correct and that his parents had randomly chosen the day.

Cole put the file back in its place in the drawer and then was stumped about what to do next. *Was there another baby with burn marks?* He clearly remembered the agency administrator talking about "Charles" when he'd witnessed his parents meeting with her.

"The file you're looking for is Whitten."

Cole turned to see the man in the black cloak and white mask standing on the other side of the table.

"Whitten?" Cole asked.

"I was adopted by Gregory and Gayle Whitten."

Cole shone the flashlight at his brother. "Why don't you take off your mask?"

"I always wear it. The burn damage is too…let's just say that I could play the role of the Phantom of the Opera without any stage makeup."

Cole started to sweat. He didn't know if he was dreaming or what….

"I have imagined you for a long time," he said. "When we were little, you didn't have on a mask or have burns on your face."

Charlie cocked his head slightly. "Aren't you imagining me now?"

Cole didn't know if he was or not. All this time-jumping and Dream States stuff all blended together into a confusing and unpleasant jumble. Instead of answering the question, Cole turned to the filing cabinets, found the drawer marked W, and pulled it out. Sure enough, there was a file marked WHITTEN. Cole returned to the table, sat, and opened the folder. A male baby boy with severe burn injuries had also been brought to the agency by the same state-run organization on what appeared to be the same day as when Cole was received, although it wasn't clear that they arrived together. Adoption took longer for little Charles. It wasn't until February 1949 that the Whittens took "Charlie" home with them. Cole noted their address as being in the Lower East Side. It was not an ideal part of the city. At the time, it was an area of low-income families, mostly immigrants. Gregory Whitten was employed as a janitor. No job was listed for Gayle. Cole imagined that Charlie had a rough upbringing.

Maybe that's why he'd become a murderer.

Oh my God, I said it. Or, rather, I thought it.

In 1969, though, the murders hadn't happened yet.

Still seated, Cole looked at his brother, who, surprisingly, still stood there against the back wall. "Charlie…are you really here in the year 1969, or are you here, like me, from the year 1985?"

"I could ask you the same question. Are you really here in 1969, or are you here from the year 1985?"

"I'm in a memory."

"Are you really?"

Cole felt a shiver run down his spine.

Then Charlie said, "You know, I've been looking for *you*, too. We have a connection. We were in the womb together. Did you know I hated you then?"

"You hated me in the *womb*? How is that possible?"

"I hated you then, and I hate you now. You've had a good life, and I haven't. I think I'm going to end yours."

"I didn't have a good life at all. I've been miserable for most of it. I've even played Russian Roulette, probably hoping the magic bullet would come up. And, besides, you *did* end my life. You killed me in 1985."

Charlie grinned beneath the white mask, which covered only the top half of his face. "Perhaps you can try and stop me from doing that."

A woman's scream in the distance startled Cole. He turned his head toward the door. "What was that?" He then looked back at his brother…who wasn't there…

… And then neither was he. The RECORDS room at the orphanage faded into nothingness as Cole's consciousness returned to his Hotel Destiny office. He was still sitting behind his desk, an empty glass and a half-full bottle of Jack Daniel's in front of him.

The woman's scream, however, was real, and it was coming from Laurence Flynn's old office, just down the hall from his own.

20

Cole jumped from his seat and ran into the corridor outside his office. He immediately knew that he was once again in a different time and year. The screaming was indeed coming from Laurence Flynn's old office—the manager's abode.

There was a startling crash that shook the walls, and then the door flew open and Miranda Flynn emerged. She was not yet the overweight Miranda he had seen in 1948 in the apartment bedroom with the cribs, so it was surely an earlier year in the timeline. Something was terribly wrong, though. She had a bloody nose and her face was red—from being hit, most likely.

"I *hate* you!" she yelled back into the office and then ran into the employee stairwell by the dumbwaiter.

Curly Chadwick stormed out of the office after her. "Come back here! I'm talking to you! Don't you run away from me!" Despite Chadwick's size and bulk, he was surprisingly agile and quick on his feet. At first, he was unsure where Miranda had fled. He peered into the lobby from behind the reception desk and barked at the employee there, "Where did she go?" The underling, trembling with fear, pointed to the employee stairwell. Chadwick bolted for it and disappeared inside.

Cole had been frozen in place during all this, but now he leapt into action. He couldn't let that brute hit his mother again. He opened the stairwell door and followed the gangster up the flight to the kitchen. When he got there, the staff were cowering against the walls as Miranda picked up a china coffee cup and threw it at Chadwick. He dodged it and it crashed against a cabinet next to Cole.

"You're not to so much as *look* at another man!" Chadwick shouted at her.

"Go to hell, Curly! Leave me alone!"

He lunged across the space at her, but she managed to avoid him, pick up a large cutting knife, and hold it defensively in front of her. "Stay away, Curly! Leave me alone!"

"I saw you making eyes at him! What's going on between you two? Huh? Answer me!"

She made stabbing motions with the knife. "I'll cut you, Curly, I swear I will!"

"Oh, you're going to cut me, are you? Just try, slut! That's what you are! You're a slut!"

"HEY!"

Cole shouted at them, not knowing if he was visible or not. Chadwick, though, flinched and turned to him. "Who the hell are you?"

Yep. He was visible. Miranda focused on him, her eyes wild with terror and anger, and then confusion. The crease in her brow indicated she recognized him...from *somewhere*.

"I'm the hotel detective!" Cole announced. "Leave her alone."

"You're not the goddamned hotel detective. I don't know who the hell you are." The big man moved forward with the force of a bull, but Cole was ready for him. His years of boxing lessons, bar brawling, and New York street smarts paid off.

Cole delivered a powerful sledgehammer punch to Chadwick's nose. The man's head bobbed, he blinked several times, and then he lost his balance and fell backward to the floor. He wasn't down for the count, though. The tough guy immediately started to get up, but Cole moved in and kicked Chadwick in the jaw. The gangster's skull slammed hard into the tile floor...and he was out.

Cole looked around. The staff had fled the kitchen, but he zoomed in on a calendar affixed to the wall near the food preparation area. March 1946.

1946? Really?

Miranda stood in front of him with the knife still in her hand, breathing heavily, her eyes bulging at what she had just witnessed. Blood was still seeping out of her nose, covering her mouth and chin. Cole glanced at the kitchen sink, saw a wet cloth, and grabbed it. He moved toward Miranda, saying, "Here, put this on your—"

"Keep away from me!" she spat.

Cole held up his arms, the rag limp in his hand. "I mean you no harm, Miranda. You're bleeding."

"I know you, don't I! How do I know you?"

"We've…met a few times before."

She backed away a few feet, genuinely frightened of him. "I do remember you. You were at the New Year's Eve party. We *danced* together. When was that? When was that?"

"New Year's Eve going into 1936."

Miranda spoke accusatorially, as if he had done something horrible. "And I saw you before that! When I was a teenager! Right?"

"Yes. That was 1930. We're going to see each other again in 1948."

"You look the same! What are you? *What are you?* Are you one of the ghosts? Are you a *ghost?* Don't come near me!"

Cole continued to hold up his hands. "I just want to help." He gestured with his head toward the unconscious Chadwick on the floor. "Miranda, you need to get away from this man. He's running a brothel out of the hotel and he's involved in other organized crime activities."

She made a face and spit out her words. "I know that! Get out of here before his lapdogs find you here and see what you've done. They'll kill you first and ask questions later!"

Ha. I'm already dead, so that's not going to work.

As if on cue, Shake—Chadwick's right-hand man—and two other heavies burst into the kitchen from the stairwell. There was a moment suspended in time as the men saw their boss on the floor, the boss' girlfriend with a bloody nose and a knife, and a stranger in a tuxedo who appeared to be the instigator of whatever had happened.

Shake removed a gun from a shoulder holster under his jacket.

Cole spun and threw the wet cloth into Shake's face. The pistol went off, propelling a round into the floor, but then Shake clumsily dropped the weapon. Cole acted quickly, bounded over Chadwick, who was beginning to stir with accompanying groans, and then slugged the man nearest to the stairwell door. With him tumbling away, Cole was able to dart out of the kitchen before the men could register what had just occurred.

Now, which way to go? Traverse the access corridor to the ballroom foyer, or go through the swinging doors to the ballroom itself?

He chose the latter and rushed into the empty Grand Room, where chairs were stacked on top of tables, as they always were between events. As he ran across the dance floor, he realized what a mistake he'd made. The only way out was to the foyer anyway, but by the time he decided to reverse course, the men had erupted into the ballroom behind him. Guns blazed and filled the room with surprisingly loud, reverberating chaos.

Cole pushed over one of the tables so that it sat on edge, the top perpendicular to the floor. The chairs went flying. He skirted around and used the tabletop as cover, hiding him from view.

No one can see me! Be invisible! he willed. *I'm a ghost! I can't be seen!*

"Look, he went behind that table!"

"What is he, stupid?"

"Come out from behind there, buster!" Shake shouted.

Cole sat in a fetal position, his arms covering his head.

Uh oh...

With three guns pointed in front of them, the men moved around to the other side of the table and fired, delivering several rounds of hot lead...and then the barrage abruptly stopped.

"Hey! He's not here!"

"What happened to him?"

"He went behind this table! I saw him! You saw him, right?"

"Yeah, I saw him."

"Then where'd he go?"

The men looked around, completely baffled.

"The boss ain't going to like this."

"Come on, let's keep looking for him."

One man continued to search the ballroom, although it was clear their prey wasn't in there. The other two headed out the doors to the foyer.

Cole had felt the bullets hit his body, but there had been no pain. He patted himself, looked down, touched where the *thumps* had struck him, and his clothing was perfectly intact.

Whaaaat?

He turned his head to look at the tabletop. It was perforated with eight bullet holes. The rounds had gone right through him.

Holy shit. So that's *what happens if I'm shot. Jesus, I'm invincible!*

No, he thought again. That wasn't true. He was dead. As dead as roadkill on the side of a highway. Dead as a gazelle in the jaws of a lion. Dead as a mummy in a pharaoh's tomb. Dead as....

Stop it. You're being ridiculous.

Cole stood and brushed off his tux. As he left the ballroom, he thought about what he had witnessed. In 1946, apparently things were not rosy in the Chadwick household. He couldn't recall if Miranda had married him—Cole didn't think so. They had lived together in Room 302 beginning in 1933, when Chadwick helped Miranda re-open the hotel, through 1948, when a fire broke out in the apartment, killing her. What had happened to Curly? Cole couldn't remember, or perhaps he didn't know.

He had seen early on that their relationship was based on money and opportunity rather than any kind of genuine affection on Miranda's part. Perhaps it was a sign of the times, the Great Depression and all that. Women had been forced to depend on men, whether it was an abusive arrangement or not.

The fact that she was his birth mother made it doubly worse. Cole felt sorry for her and wished he could do something about it. Unfortunately, he was coming to realize that he couldn't change a damned thing in the timeline of history. He had no influence whatsoever. All he could do was observe and learn.

"Find your heritage," Agnieszka had said.

It wasn't called Hotel Destiny for nothing.

21

Still unseen, Cole left the ballroom as Chadwick's bozos continued to search for him. Frustrated and angry, Cole decided that he needed some fresh air. From the twelfth floor, one was able to use the fire escape stairwell to climb the steps, open a hatch, and walk out onto the roof. Would that be accessible? He hadn't been able to physically leave the building—the hurricane-like black winds always prevented him from doing so. Would they strike on top of the hotel? Only one way to find out.

Cole rang for the elevator, but riding the cars was risky. There was a portal in one of the two cars—and he'd already forgotten which one—and other bizarre things had happened when he'd stepped into the lift. This time, the gold doors opened, he stepped in and reached to press the button for the twelfth floor...and he hesitated.

See? Weird things always happen in these goddamned elevators!

For the first time in his experience at Hotel Destiny, there was a button for a thirteenth floor. However, the indicators above the doors still went up only to "12."

Fine. What the hell....

He pressed the button and the doors closed. The lift behaved normally as it ascended to the top of the building. The floor indicators lit up as he passed each successive one..."4," "5," "6".... Finally, the number "12" illuminated, but the elevator kept moving. A few seconds later, it stopped.

The doors opened to what appeared to be a hall of guest rooms, just like all the other floors in the hotel.

Cole stepped out of the elevator...

... and the noise of the helicopter was deafening in his

ears. Fully equipped with a heavy backpack, helmet, and a brand new M16 A1 rifle, Cole landed feet first on the ground after performing a short jump from the Bell UH-1D Iroquois' fuselage with nine other members of his squad. He instinctively ran low as the chopper remained "light on the skids." It had landed long enough for the crewman to yell, "Belts," followed by the men shouting the same thing in unison and unbuckling their seat belts. "Go!" was the next command, and the men had moved single file toward the front of the chopper and propelled themselves out the door. As the troops exited, the weight of the aircraft decreased and it rose a little. This allowed the pilot to fly out fast after dropping the men into the combat zone.

Holy shit, I'm back in Vietnam! I do NOT want to be here. I do NOT want to be here!

But he was.

The year had to be late 1969 or early 1970, when he was in the thick of it, assigned to a platoon in the 25th Infantry Division of the U.S. Army.

He had no idea what precise spot or mission he was on. Those years were all a blur to Cole. If you saw one part of the jungle, you saw it all. Up ahead, the trees and foliage were on fire. The sound of battle was in the near distance, not too far away. The *rat-tat-tat* of M16s and other weapons created a cacophony that was a soundtrack to Cole's nightmares for many years following his discharge.

"How you doing over there, buddy?"

Cole looked to see who had spoken as they ran toward the "shit." It was Tim! Tim Busby, his best and only friend in the army. While Cole had tended to remain a loner and had a reputation for being anti-social, Tim did, too, so it was natural that they had formed a bond.

"Where are we, again?" Cole shouted. "I've already forgotten the mission!"

Tim laughed. "You kill me, Cole!"

I won't kill you, Tim. A boobytrap in Cambodia will. Not now, but later in the war. I will witness it, too, and it will be horrible.

The Sergeant First Class, whose name Cole couldn't recall, signaled for the squad to hunker down at the edge of where the jungle became thick. Smoke from the fires made for tough visibility. The heat was unbearable, as the sun was beating down on them at what appeared to be twelve o'clock high. The ground was wet, though, as the jungle floor tended to be, and Cole remembered how he would sometimes grasp the cool mud and squeeze it, just to get a sense that not everything around him was in an oven. He did so now as the sergeant barked.

"The platoon is pinned-down about a klick away. Our job is to reinforce. Let's go, and if you see anything not dressed in a U.S. army uniform, *kill it*!"

The men shouted an affirmative, the sarge waved them on, and they began to move through the dense brush. Cole felt as if he were on autopilot, going through the motions, following the maneuvers of Tim and his fellow grunts.

Why am I here? What "lesson" am I supposed to learn revisiting this godforsaken place?

Still, the familiar sensation of being totally *alert* was back. Being in Vietnam was like a 24/7 hit of cocaine. Every nerve ending was always ready to ignite, even in those moments when he managed to get some precious sleep. It was a continuous psychedelic whirlwind of noise, sweat, heat, and violence.

They ran from cover to cover, keeping an eye out for figures darting through the forest. It wasn't long, though, before the men came upon the first group of corpses. First there were two. Then there were five. When they found seven other dead soldiers dressed in U.S. army gear, the men knew they were too late.

"Where's Charlie now?" Tim asked rhetorically.

Cole did a double-take. *Charlie? My brother?* Then he realized Tim was talking about the Viet Cong—the nickname the army had given them was "Charlie."

"It was a hit and run," the sergeant said. "They can't be far. We heard the gunfire. Spread out and find those fuckers! Shoot 'em in the back if you have to!"

The squad did as it was told. As Cole moved farther into the jungle, the scenario was coming back to him. It was the fall of 1969 and he had been "in country" for three months. This had been one of his first serious excursions with the squad. He had arrived in Nam around the time that morale among U.S. troops was rapidly declining. He had witnessed firsthand a unit "sand-bagging," an act in which the men, ordered to go on patrol, would simply find a comfortable place to sit it out and radio in false reports. "Search and Destroy" missions sometimes became "Search and Avoid." Cole, on the other hand, took his role seriously. While he hated Vietnam and the constant threat of death, he soon found that his motivation to enlist had been sound. The army *did* teach him discipline. It *did* give him a purpose, whereas the years following high school graduation had been aimless and dangerous. Moreover, the war gave Cole an outlet through which he could channel his anger.

He took out his rage on the enemy, and he now recalled that *this* mission was when he first realized it.

Within minutes of the sergeant's command, Cole noticed four figures running away from him not far ahead. He picked up his speed, and then saw that a rise in terrain to his left might provide him with an advantage. Cole scampered up the squatty hill, and this gave him a clearer view of the four soldiers in retreat.

They were Viet Cong. One of them was equipped with a flamethrower.

Cole lifted his M16, aimed, and picked off each man, one by one.

When he was done, Cole moved down the knoll and went to examine his handiwork. The shots had been clean and deadly. It had been too easy.

The sergeant, Tim, and another man came running up to him.

"Good work, private! Let's keep searching."

Tim laughed. "We're going to start calling you Killer Cole!"

That was the first time he'd been dubbed by that nickname. It had stuck, and several of the men often called him Killer Cole from then on. He had accepted it, but he didn't really care for it.

"Let me shake your hand, pal." Tim held out his palm. Cole reached out to grab it and…

…he took the joint Tim was offering.

The scene had shifted.

Cole was now inside what he recognized to be his old barracks. It was nighttime. Rock music was playing on an 8-track player. Jimi Hendrix's "Voodoo Child." He had a can of Pabst Blue Ribbon in one hand, and Tim's doobie in the other. Christmas lights had been strung around their home-away-from-home at Tây Ninh Combat Base, which sat approximately twelve kilometers from the Vietnam-Cambodia border.

Faces he knew were around him, but the names were elusive. They were drinking beer and harder liquor, smoking pot, and having a little R&R. Two guys were shooting up.

The time-hopping was more than disorienting, especially when it involved skipping to locations such as Vietnam. Cole remembered this Christmas party of 1969, though. He was already inebriated and had trouble breathing in the smoke-filled barracks.

"No, thanks," he said to Tim as he handed the marijuana cigarette back. He wasn't much of a pot smoker. In fact, Cole never did go in for drugs other than alcohol. He examined the beer he was holding and recalled how the cans back then were "flat tops"—they had to be opened with a can opener, or "church key," before pop tops were the norm. The soldiers usually had American-brewed brands to drink, such as Pabst or Budweiser, but every now and then he'd try the local Vietnamese stuff, Ba Moui Ba, or "33," as it was called. The quality was decidedly under par.

"I need some air," he mumbled.

"What?" Tim gasped on the inhale.

"I said I need some air! I'm going outside."

"You want me to come with?"

"Nah. I want to be alone."

Cole left the noisy quarters and walked out onto the hard dirt. A party was going on in all the barracks. The various strains of rock music blended to form an ambient rumble that was somewhat comforting. The army upper brass had turned a blind eye to the booze and the drugs. They were probably having their own celebration. It was Christmas. Ho ho ho.

The stars shone brightly in the night sky. There was no moon. The air was chilly, but nighttime in the jungle regions was always colder than one expected.

Cole walked past the 45th Surgical Hospital, where the surgeons and doctors and patients were surely also enjoying a drink or toke or two. He moved away from the barracks, closer to the chopper landing zone, found a grouping of discarded crates, and sat down.

What am I doing here? How do I get back to the hotel? Do I even want to go back to the hotel?

It was all such a drag, being dead.

"Do you like it when they call you Killer Cole?"

Cole turned to the voice, and there he was. Charlie, in his black cloak and white mask, sitting a few feet away on another crate.

"No," he answered. "Not really."

"Don't lie. You like it."

"I'm not a killer, except here. In the army. It's my job."

"If you say so, pal."

"You're the killer, Charlie. You're the one killing those people at the hotel, aren't you?"

"What hotel?"

"Hotel Destiny. Come on."

"I don't know what you're talking about," Charlie said. "This is 1969. You don't work at the hotel yet."

That confused Cole. After a moment he attempted to rationalize it, more to himself than to Charlie. "This is a *memory.* I'm looking back at all this. I'm in my body *then.* I'm re-living it."

"Am *I* a memory?" Charlie asked.

"I don't know what you are. But I'm going to find you back in *my* time, and I'm going to stop you from killing those people."

"Good luck with that. Oh—by the way...pretty soon you will have a psychotic episode and spend two months in the hospital in Saigon."

"What?"

That's when a massive explosion kicked him hard and sent him flying into the air...

22

...and he landed hard in the mud, which cushioned the impact. He curled up to protect himself, but the sequence of blasts eventually halted.

Now *where am I?*

Frightened out of his wits, Cole looked around and saw Tim and other members of his squad hunkered down, hoping for the best.

Tim was near hysterics. "Oh, Lord, oh my God! We're going to die! We're going to die!"

"Shut up, private!" the sarge forcefully whispered.

That's when Cole knew what had happened. Another time shift had placed him on a night patrol in the jungle. It was May 1970, and the platoon was part of several U.S. missions that infiltrated Cambodia in order to seek out and destroy suspected Communist military headquarters and confiscate their supplies. The operation focused on the southern part of Cambodia known as the "Fishhook" because of its shape, and history would show that it was a bloody two months between May and June of that year.

The men heard the enemy shouting in their language, taunting them up ahead in the brush. Cole recalled the translation as something like, "Come and get us, White Invader!"

Tim unhooked a grenade from his belt, rose to his feet, pulled the pin with his teeth, and threw the explosive as far as he could into the darkness. A few seconds later, it detonated.

Then there was silence.

"I think I got him!" Tim whispered to the sergeant.

But then the shout returned. "Come and get us, White Invader!"

Tim winced and sunk back down into the mud.

Nevertheless, the gunfire had ceased. Except for the lone man hollering into the night sky, it was as if the squad was alone.

"Men," the sergeant relayed, "we're pushing ahead! On my command, get ready..." Every soldier got to their feet but kept themselves in a bent, squatting position. "...and...GO GO GO!"

They were off and running toward the voice, which was still shouting. Cole realized that this was the night Tim would buy the farm. He wanted to stop his friend and keep him from moving forward, but he figured—*What's the use? I can't change what's going to happen. I know that now.*

The anticipation of what he was about to see—and couldn't avoid seeing it—was terrifying.

Another explosion shook the trees just twenty meters to their left. The men once again crouched to cover themselves as debris and embers rained around their positions.

"GO GO GO!" the sergeant commanded again once the eruption had settled, and they were off. The jungle wasn't as dense as some of the places where they'd been in Vietnam, but it was still dark and difficult to navigate around trees and foliage that blended into the shadows.

"Come and get us, White Invader!"

Cole lost sight of Tim as he pushed forward. He knew that the enemy was not far away, but he was also aware of the tragedy that was about to strike his buddy.

Damn it.

He broke off the trajectory he was on and moved to the left. "Tim!" he called out in a loud whisper. "Tim!"

Movement nearby jerked and halted. "Here!"

I have to try and stop it. Even if it doesn't work, I have to try.

"Keep moving!" the sergeant commanded.

Cole grabbed Tim. "Don't go that way. Come this way with me."

"What, are you scared?" Tim laughed. "You're Killer Cole! You don't need me to hold your hand, pal."

The sergeant spotted them and barked, "What's the problem? Get moving, ladies!"

"Yes, sir!" Tim replied and leaped forward. Cole couldn't stop him. Instead, he followed his tracks, just as he had really done in May 1970.

More gunfire broke out ahead. They heard a scream, and it wasn't the enemy.

Cole dreaded it…he kept saying to himself, *Don't let it happen again, don't let it happen again.*

As they approached the melee, Cole wondered why he hadn't yet heard the dreadful blast. Then he realized—the time of the explosion had come and gone! Tim had not stepped on the boobytrap after all! It should have occurred somewhere *back there*, but it didn't! Had he been successful in delaying him just enough that Tim had altered his footsteps, sending him a few feet out of the way so that he missed it?

BOOOM!

Cole stopped running.

No. He hadn't stopped it.

He had just seen for the second time his friend blown in half, the man's blood and organs becoming projectiles for yards around.

Cole dropped to his knees and beat the ground.

Then he remembered what would happen next.

Oh, my God….

The boobytrap had also acted as an alarm. The enemy knew the squad was nearby and in the bull's eye. The combatants unleashed a flurry of incendiary payload that made the squad think they were falling into the pits of hell. Cole would learn later that the Viet Cong had used RPG-2 grenade launchers in a calculated, simultaneous attack. Half of Cole's squad was killed, several men were wounded, and Cole screamed as the firebombs burst around him. The trees were suddenly on fire and the brush was a flaming orange terror-ball.

Fire!

Cole dreaded it more than anything on the earth.

He felt pain in his left leg, hip, and side, even though physically he was not burning—yet.

Cole panicked and bolted from his position, but he couldn't

run anywhere. The flames encircled him. There was no opening.

He continued to yell. He believed that now, as he had been convinced then, it was all over. He thrashed on the ground, rolling in the mud, thinking that his uniform was smoldering, and he needed to put it out.

Room 302 of Hotel Destiny. 1948.

Burning.

Screams.

His mother....

Flames are scorching my skin!

Suddenly, hands were over Cole. "Hold still, we're getting you out of here!" a man hollered. But Cole fought and wrestled and continued to cry in anguish and horror.

"Stop it, man! You're not on fire!"

It was no use, he was *burning, burning, burning...!*

"I can't hold him! Medic!"

Leave me alone! I'm dying here, can't you see? The fire is all over me!

"He's going nuts! Hold him down!"

Cole felt the needle puncture his leg. He slugged the man who'd given him the shot.

"Ow! Goddamn it! *Hold him!*"

Then things got cloudy. The fire started to fade away. Cole began to feel light, as if he were floating. No, the men were carrying him. Loading him on a stretcher. *What's happening, guys? Wait, what...?...*

... And the cacophony of war that was ringing in his ears abruptly halted. In its place was the slow *creak...creak...creak* of some sort of machine nearby.

Cole felt as if he was waking from a deep sleep.

Creak...creak...creak....

What was that sound? It was annoying.

He opened his eyes.

Daylight. White sheets. A slow-turning fan on the ceiling.

That's it! That's what's making the noise!

Creak...creak...creak....

Cole recalled that he had hated that squeaky fan.

He was in the army hospital in Saigon. July 1970.

"... because of his breakdown, I'm not sure he'll be fit to return to active duty."

The voice was that of a doctor. Cole turned his head slightly and attempted to focus his eyes. Yep. A man with a white lab coat was talking to an army officer.

"Private Sackler suffered a serious mental and emotional breakdown. He believes he was burned badly on a mission, although he wasn't. There are indeed long-healed burn wounds on parts of his body that probably occurred when he was a child. That might have something to do with it. A psychological reaction to the combat he was in. Maybe he had a repressed memory of being burned."

"I don't believe in that 'repressed memory' shit," the officer said. "Is he going to get well, or do we have to send him home?"

"It's my recommendation that this soldier be medically discharged."

It was the "psychotic episode" Charlie had warned him about. Cole vividly recalled it, and it was no fun re-living it.

The next memory Cole had was that of a nurse helping him out of bed. He got to his feet, stepped forward...

... and he was smoothly and inexplicably back in the elevator in Hotel Destiny, exiting the car. He was exactly where he had been when he'd hopped back to his remembrances in Vietnam. He had been planning to go to the hotel roof to get some fresh air. Earlier there had been the impossible thirteenth floor that didn't exist, but now he was standing on the twelfth floor, the proper highest level in the hotel.

Dare he continue?

23

Cole confirmed that he was indeed on the twelfth floor, and then he stepped back into the stairwell to ascend the short flight to the small platform above his head. A door there opened to the roof. Sometimes maintenance men had to go up there to repair a/c and heating units that were positioned on top of the hotel.

He opened the door, moved through it, and he was twelve stories above the street in New York City. It was a clear but very chilly night. The waning gibbous moon shone behind a few clouds along with the twinkling stars that managed to poke through. He was getting good at detecting that there had been yet another change in the year.

There was music and the noise of a crowd in the distance. He moved across the roof to the northeast corner, where he could view Times Square from above. A huge throng of people were gathered there, and a small orchestra was set up in a bandstand. There was an abundance of balloons and streamers, and a gigantic wrought iron ball was about to drop. He caught a glimpse of several banners that proclaimed that this was New Year's Eve...and New York was about to usher in the year 1948. Cole's birth year.

Cole looked over the ledge that surrounded the roof. The street down below was packed with cars and people, but it would be quite easy to climb up, approach the edge, and jump. Surprisingly, considering the history of Hotel Destiny, he knew of no instances in which anyone had taken a suicide leap from the roof.

Hey. Something's missing!

The black, hurricane-like winds were not battering him.

That happened only when he tried to leave through a door on the street level. Here? Nothing. He supposed that if he really tried to jump off the building, only then would the winds blow in and prevent him from doing the deed. Still, that was only speculation. Perhaps he *could* jump! Should he try?

You're thinking nutty stuff, Cole Sackler. But what harm could it do? I'm already dead, right?

Cole stared at the ground below for some time before he eventually decided to let it go. If he were going to be stuck in the hotel for eternity as a ghost, there would be other opportunities when he could try it. Not tonight, though.

He gazed out over the metropolis with its magnificent skyscrapers dotted with pinpricks of light. Who was behind those windows? What were they doing? Not many people had televisions then, so were they listening to the big countdown on the radio? Were husbands getting ready to kiss their wives and wish them, "Happy New Year?"

Seeing the cityscape at night reminded Cole of when he had returned from Vietnam in the early fall of 1970. This was exactly how it had looked, for he had ridden the taxi into town around midnight. The next few years after that were a bit of a blur. He'd gone to see his adoptive parents, but his mother was sick, and his father didn't really want him around. She died of cancer in early '72. Cole and his father didn't see each other much after that—maybe an occasional cup of coffee together, but no more than once a year.

Cole had found a cheap studio apartment in SoHo and worked menial jobs. Dishwasher. Waiter. Newspaper vendor. The best one was when he landed the position of assistant to a rather sleazy private investigator who chased ambulances and followed cheating spouses. Cole had been responsible for taking revealing photos that clinched some of his boss' cases. The P.I. was a drunk, and that ended up being a bad influence on Cole, who had been relatively sober while he was in the army. There had been the beer, and lots of it, but he had managed to stay away from whiskey and vodka and other harder fare while he was overseas. By 1971, though, Cole was drinking again. Then, in 1972, he had experienced his first Dream State since his breakdown in the jungle. The Dream States—the "blackouts"—had rarely occurred since he was a teenager, so it was always a welcome surprise when he had a pleasant one. Had the freak-out in Vietnam been a "bad" Dream State? He didn't know. Mostly, they sent him back to agreeable memories. The one from '72 was different. He didn't remember anything about it, except that he'd woken up one morning in his apartment and a week had passed. He was malnourished and dehydrated, and he'd had no idea what had happened to him. Very bizarre.

All that changed in 1974, when he had applied for the job as night manager at Hotel Destiny. J. T. Dunlap, a boisterous, overweight, and most likely mob-connected real estate tycoon, had advertised in the *Village Voice*, and Cole went for it. His experience as a soldier, as an assistant to a P.I., and his obvious New York street smarts landed him the position. Dunlap had purchased the property from Miranda Flynn's estate in 1951. By the '70s, the hotel was a dump, a place where no "respectable" tourist would stay, and Dunlap capitalized on it. With cheap rooms, no amenities, and probably kickbacks from the unsavory types who populated the area, Dunlap made a profit on the place. He kept the employee payroll down (Cole could count on two hands the number of people who worked at the hotel at any given time), but he didn't bother keeping the crime out. Dunlap had told him, "Just make sure no one gets killed in the joint. You're the hotel detective now."

Cole had been unable to keep that promise. Ironically, there hadn't been any unnatural deaths in the place in the 1950s or '60s. One old man had had a heart attack in the hotel in 1957, a woman had fallen down the stairs and broken her neck in 1963, and another man had simply checked into a room to die in 1967. The first *murder* since Theresa Flynn's had occurred in 1972, when a maid was shot in the basement boiler room. Cole now knew that this was Agnieszka.

What was her last name? I heard Sergeant Redenius say it. Oh, yeah. Preisner. Agnieszka Preisner.

That was, of course, before Cole was employed there. Unfortunately, it was on his watch that Hutch Butler, Cindy Walker, Chantel Lee, and Martine Crawford had been shot, all by, presumably, the same handgun. The killer's signature.

Since his own death, Cole had revisited the crime scenes of Butler, Walker, and Crawford. What about Chantal Lee?

She was killed in 1982, not long after Cole's divorce. He had already begun living at the hotel in the empty office that was connected to his…

…"When did she check in to the hotel?" Sergeant Redenius asked.

Cole answered, "Last night, about eleven o'clock. I was at the front desk."

He then looked around and found that he was no longer on the roof. Instead, Cole was standing in the hallway of the ninth floor, outside Room 907.

Here we go again. Another memory thingy.

"Were you the only employee at the hotel?" Redenius asked.

"Uh, yeah."

"Really? A twelve-story hotel, and there's one person in the whole goddamn building that works here?"

"Talk to Mr. Dunlap, Sarge. I don't do the hiring and firing or make the schedules."

"No wonder you hide in your office and drink all night."

"Excuse me?"

Redenius slapped Cole on the shoulder and laughed. "Sorry, Sackler, just breaking your balls. You know this is the fourth homicide we've had in the hotel in ten years?"

"Is it some kind of record?" Cole asked, unable to disguise the sarcasm.

"Actually, no. In this precinct, I've seen worse. Still…."

Redenius turned away and went into the room. Cole couldn't prevent his morbid curiosity from acting up. He followed the cop inside to join the rest of the team that was processing the scene.

Chantal Lee was an Asian woman of maybe nineteen or twenty. Pretty. Thin. An autopsy would later reveal that she was not an addict. Why she was in the hotel was a mystery. Whatever the reason, her brains had been blown away while she was standing in front of the bathroom mirror. She'd been wearing a silk robe that she'd had in her meager bag that didn't contain much else.

"Was she turning tricks?" Redenius asked.

"I have no idea."

"Yeah, you don't know much, do you, Sackler? How many other people are staying in the hotel?"

"Last I looked, fourteen rooms are booked."

"Jesus, how do you guys make any money?"

"Don't ask me."

Redenius shook his head. "I guess finding any witnesses will be a lost cause. Get me a list of the rooms. We'll knock on doors anyway and do our job."

Cole felt ill looking at the ghastly sight. He nodded at the sergeant, left, and made his way to the elevator. The policeman was correct, though. Cole had been "hiding" in his office, drinking Jack Daniel's, and drowning his sorrows over being dumped by Janine...

...The strains of "Auld Lang Syne" filtered back into his consciousness, and Cole was back on the hotel roof. The crowd below and to the northeast had just ushered in 1948.

Well, what's it going to be, Coleman Sackler? Are we going to try and jump off the building, or should we just go back inside out of the cold?

"Let's go inside," he said aloud.

Cole turned to walk across the roof back to the access door, but then he saw a figure standing near the ledge on the opposite side. He moved a little closer to discern a woman with blonde hair and wearing a fur coat. She looked as if she might be considering climbing onto the ledge, too. He moved even nearer, stepping quietly so he wouldn't startle her, and realized she was Miranda Flynn. His mother had gained quite a bit of weight since he'd last seen her in 1946. She more resembled the woman he'd seen in the bedroom with the two cribs, which was only six months away in this timeline's future. That meant she was three or four months pregnant...with him and Charlie.

He called her name softly. She turned sharply, squinted her eyes and then her mouth dropped open.

"You!"

Cole held up his hands. "I mean you no harm."

"I'm not so sure about that. You're a ghost. I know it. You

pop up every few years out of the blue. Who *are* you?"

He didn't know how much he could tell her. "You're right. I am a ghost, but I'm a friendly one."

"Are you here to stop me?"

"Stop you?"

She indicated the edge of the roof. "I was thinking about jumping."

"Why?"

"My life is in ruins."

Cole nodded. "Let me guess. Is it Curly?"

"Yes. Life with him is unbearable, and I can't get away. Oh, why am I telling you this?"

"Because I'm a ghost, remember?" She laughed a little at that. Cole could see now that she'd been drinking. "Maybe you should go back inside."

With a sigh, she kept talking. "I met a man a few months ago. He's an FBI agent. Michael Fuller. He's working undercover to investigate Curly's activities. I've been helping him, and we fell in love."

"Uh oh."

"Yeah. And that's not the worst part."

"What's the worst part?"

She took a tissue out of her coat pocket and wiped her nose. The tears had begun to flow. "I'm going to have a baby."

"I see." He let her sniffle in silence for a moment and then asked, "I take it Curly is not the father."

She shook her head. "I stopped letting Curly touch me three years ago—after that time in the kitchen. Oh, God, Curly will kill me when he finds out. He'll kill me, and he'll kill Michael, too."

Cole hesitated before asking, but then he did. "Are you carrying twins?"

She looked at him funny. "Twins?"

"It's possible you might be carrying twins."

"How do you know?"

He shrugged.

My God...now I know the identity of my real father.

"I want to meet this Michael Fuller," he said.

"Why?"

"I can tell him what I know about Curly's activities at the hotel."

Miranda pulled on her lower lip. "I don't know.... Am I supposed to tell him you're a ghost?"

"No, don't do that."

"Yeah, he might think I'm nuts. I think I'm nuts anyway, talking to you. Look, I'm supposed to see him tonight. We usually meet in one of the guest rooms, because it's real hard for me to leave the hotel when Curly's in town. His men would tell him if I left. They keep an eye on all the doors."

"How does Mr. Fuller get in?"

"Oh, he pretends he's a guest of the hotel. Well, he *is* a guest of the hotel. Everyone thinks he's an insurance salesman who comes to New York every month from out of town."

"Miranda, if he loves you, don't you think he'd feel pretty bad if you jumped off the roof?"

She nodded and started crying again. Cole realized he had a handkerchief in his tuxedo jacket pocket, so he pulled it out and handed it over. "Here."

"Thank you." She blew her nose. "I'm sorry."

"It's all right. Don't be sorry."

"You really want to meet him?"

"I do. Shall we go inside?"

She hesitated and then nodded. "All right."

He then took his mother's hand and led her across the roof to the access door.

24

Cole and Miranda took the elevator to the fourth floor. When the doors opened, she remained in the car.

"He's in Room 408. Just tell him I sent you, and that I'll be there in fifteen minutes. I need to…powder my nose." She wiped her face and watery eyes again with Cole's handkerchief. She offered it back to him.

"Keep it."

She nodded. He stepped out of the car and the doors closed.

This is going to blow my mind…I'm about to meet my father!

Cole walked down the corridor and knocked on the door to 408. After a moment, it opened to a tall, devilishly handsome man with dark hair, brown eyes, and a warm smile. He was likely in his late thirties.

"I was hoping you'd show—oh, can I help you?" The smile vanished, replaced by a crease in his brow. His eyes went up and down Cole. The tuxedo obviously threw him.

"Miranda sent me. May I come in?"

"Miranda?" His expression indicated an attempt to feign ignorance. "I'm sorry, I—"

"Mr. Fuller. Please. She'll be here in a few minutes. I have some information for you about…" Cole looked both ways down the hall and then brought his voice down. "… Curly Chadwick. *Agent* Fuller?"

Fuller's eyes narrowed. The wheels were turning. The stranger at his door knew Miranda's name, his name, his room number, and evoked the subject of his assignment. Finally, he stepped aside and said, "Come in, Mr.—?"

"Uh, Sackler. Cole Sackler." They shook hands when the door closed.

The room was designed such that there was a short corridor that contained the hall closet and led to the bedroom, which couldn't be seen fully from the door. Fuller led Cole through and to the left into the main room, which contained a queen-size bed. The bathroom was just to the left of that, placing it structurally behind the hall closet. A table and two chairs were in the corner by a window, and a dresser lined the wall opposite the bed.

"Can I offer you a drink?" The man gestured to a tray on the dresser that contained four glasses and a bottle of brandy.

Cole couldn't resist. Standing in the room with his *father* had suddenly made him very nervous and tongue-tied. A drink would help. "Sure. Thanks."

Fuller poured a couple of glasses, gave one to Cole, and then pulled out one of the chairs and tapped the back. "Have a seat, Mr. Sackler." Fuller then sat on the edge of the bed. "Cheers."

"Cheers." The brandy was good and warm after being on the roof. "And Happy New Year."

"Happy New Year to you, too. Have you been to a party?"

"A party?"

The FBI agent gestured with the glass. "Your clothes."

"Oh! Right, yeah, I was at a...party."

"Interesting style of tuxedo. Where'd you get it?"

"Oh, I, uh, it's one of those new Bohemian styles...." Cole waved a hand, dismissing the topic.

"What do you do for a living, Mr. Sackler?"

"Call me Cole. I...well, I'm a hotel detective. I'm on, uh, vacation."

"Where are you a hotel detective?"

"New Jersey."

Luckily, Fuller didn't ask what town. Instead, he went straight to, "How do you know Miranda?"

She's my birth mother. "I've known her since she was a girl. I knew her...father."

"Oh? Friend of the family's?"

"Something like that." Cole wanted to get away from talking about himself. "Look, Curly Chadwick, he's bad news. He's running all kinds of illegal activities out of the hotel."

"I know that. I just need to gather evidence and proof. You know, court of law, that sort of thing."

"Do you know about the brothel?"

Fuller's eyes narrowed again. "Do you know where it is?"

"Room 510. That's the front gate, anyway. It's possible they use other rooms on the floor, but I believe that's the place to start."

"How do you know this?"

"Observation. I've been to the hotel a few times over the years."

"Miranda didn't know where it was."

"I think Chadwick keeps a lot from her. He keeps her under his thumb in a big way. He's been known to beat her. He's a very bad man."

"I'm aware of that," Fuller said, grimacing. "That will change soon."

"I hope so."

Cole was fascinated by the man. All through the conversation, he was distracted by Fuller's looks, trying to decide how much of his features he may have inherited. In comparing what he had seen of the man and Miranda, Cole was certain that he favored his father more. This was a profound revelation to him.

"What else do you know?" his father asked.

"There are gambling operations going on higher up, on the eleventh floor. Rooms 1107, 1108, 1109, 1110...not sure where else. Poker and other high stakes games, and they handle betting for horse races, too, I imagine in Saratoga. Anyway, the eleventh floor is where that action is, at least it was a few years ago. I suppose it's possible they've moved rooms."

Fuller shook his head. "They haven't. I know about the gambling. I'm about to finish my report and send it to—" There was a knock at the door. "—ahh, that'll be Miranda. Excuse me." He got up and disappeared into the little corridor that led to the door.

Cole heard him open it, and then a male voice said, "Step back inside, G-man."

Holy shit! Is it Chadwick?

Thinking quickly, Cole jumped up, went into the bathroom,

and quietly shut the door. He then put his ear to it and listened
to the voices.

"Frisk him."

Fuller did his best to feign innocence. "What's the meaning
of this? I don't have much money if that's what you're looking
for."

"Shut up!"

"Lookee here, Shake."

"Oh, that's a nice little piece you got there, Mr. Fuller, if
that's your real name. Why would an insurance salesman carry
a gun?"

"That's everything, Shake."

"Wait. Who's in the bathroom?"

Shit! Be invisible! I'm invisible! I'm a ghost!

The door opened.

"No one, Shake. It's empty."

Cole could now view the bedroom. Shake had a gun trained
on Fuller, and one other man had the agent in a neck lock. A
third man, also armed, was checking out the bathroom.

They couldn't see him! Cole imagined that Fuller was
frightened and on high alert, but probably also bewildered as to
what had happened to his visitor.

"Come on, Fuller," Shake said. "The boss wants to see you.
Take it nice and easy going downstairs." Goon Number Two
released the neck lock. Fuller took a moment to compose himself,
and then the men marched their captive out of the room and
slammed the door shut. Cole emerged from the bathroom and
then waited a beat before opening the door again as quietly as
possible. He slipped into the hallway and watched as the four
men approached the elevator and waited for the car.

"Hey!" Cole shouted, just to make sure he was still unseen
and silent. None of them turned around. He hurried to catch up
with the group and, as the elevator doors opened, he scooted
into the car behind them and scrunched himself into a corner.
Shake pushed the "B" button—the basement. That didn't bode
well for Fuller.

What can I do? How can I stop this?

If only he had the weapon from his office downstairs, his

beloved Smith & Wesson that he'd bought after his release from the army. It was sitting in his desk drawer...but only after the year 1974.

The basement was a dark and dank place in the hotel, and it always had been. It had a catacombs-like ambiance and there were some areas which could easily double as dungeons. It had always been a creepy place. The laundry room was the closest space to the elevators. Three washers and two dryers handled the linen throughout the hotel, and a lowly employee, usually a maid, oversaw the job every day. A storage room, complete with a locking sliding door, was the largest part on the subterranean level. Spare guest room furniture, complete and in pieces, was kept there, along with decorations and accoutrements for annual ballroom events. The two paintings of the Flynns had been stored there during Cole's tenure as night manager. A ramp and loading dock pull-down steel door to the alley behind the hotel connected to the storage space. Throughout the basement were various pipes and tanks and machinery that operated the building's utilities, and the boiler room was a closed-off cell with a locking metal door. The low-pressure boiler itself was a decades-old monster that plugged along faithfully 24/7 and made a rumbling, loud *chug-chug* noise. The thing produced a lot of heat; hence, the isolation and insulation from the rest of the basement.

The trio of thugs forced Fuller past the laundry facilities, around a jog, down a short hall, and stopped at the closed boiler room door. Shake produced a key and unlocked it. Cole attempted to get around the men, but the passageway was narrow and crowded. They were in front of him and there was nothing he could do. They pushed Fuller into the room and then followed him inside.

SLAM. CLICK.

Cole hadn't realized the same key could lock the boiler room door from the inside as well. He was stuck outside, and his father was in there with the hoodlums. He examined the keyhole and felt around the frame.

I thought ghosts could slip through keyholes and under doors! All those movies and cartoons just made up that shit!

He had to go get Miranda. Maybe she could do something. Or should he call the police? That was it. Go upstairs and call the cops.

Cole turned to run back to the elevators, but the bulky frame of Curly Chadwick, with another of his henchmen, blocked the way. Chadwick moved past him and banged on the boiler room door with his fist. After a moment, it swung open. Cole got a glimpse of Michael Fuller tied to a chair as Chadwick entered, saying, "So *you're* the bastard!" The door slammed shut and was locked once again.

Cole bolted for the elevators. One car was sitting there with its doors open. He got inside and pushed the button for the third floor.

Be visible. I can be seen and heard now.

He arrived, rushed to Room 302, and banged on the door. "Miranda! Miranda! Are you in there?"

Silence.

Cole hurried down the hallway to the stairwell, scampered up the stairs to the fourth floor, and, sure enough, there she was outside of Fuller's room.

"Miranda!"

She looked at him. "Do you know where—?"

He ran to her and grabbed her by the arms. "Curly's got him down in the boiler room! He knows, Miranda!"

"Oh, my God!"

Together they turned and dashed to the elevators. Cole pressed a button and they waited for one of the cars. "Come on...." he muttered to the gold doors. Then, to her: "I'd better phone the police."

"There's no time! I want you to come with me. We have to help Michael."

The lift finally came. They got in together, he pushed the B button, and down they went. When it arrived, they moved through the labyrinth and came upon Curly opening the storage room sliding door. His men were next to him, carrying the body of a man wrapped in a blanket. Michael Fuller's bloody head poked out of one end of the roll. His eyes were closed.

Cole knew immediately what was happening—they were

going to take the corpse out through the loading dock, stuff it into a car trunk, and then dump it somewhere.

"No!" Miranda screamed.

"Get her out of here!" Chadwick barked to Shake.

"You killed my father!" Cole screamed at the gangster.

Chadwick winced. "Who the hell are you? What are you— wait, I know you! I've seen you before. What are you doing with my girl?" He pulled a gun out of his jacket, and without asking any more questions, aimed it at Cole and fired.

BANG! BANG! BANG!

The bullets perforated Cole's chest with three hard *thumps*, just as they had done before when he'd been shot. The force of the attack knocked him to the floor. Miranda shrieked again and ran to Fuller's body, which the men had dropped.

"Get her out of here!" Chadwick commanded again.

Two of them grabbed the now-hysterical woman and dragged her away and back to the elevators.

Cole, in the meantime, managed to stand up. Chadwick and the two remaining hoods stared at him wide-eyed.

"Grab him!"

They rushed him, and Cole did his best to fight. A powerhouse punch to a face, a blow to a belly—but it was no use this time. Both men locked strong arms around him and held him tightly so that Chadwick could approach, pull back a fist, and ram it into Cole's face.

Cole saw stars. *That* he'd felt. He knew it would hurt in the short term, but in the long run there would be no physical damage.

"Is he wearing a bullet-proof vest?" Chadwick asked.

Shake frisked Cole. "No, just this monkey suit."

"Weapons?"

"Nothing, boss."

"Put him in the boiler room," Chadwick said. "We'll deal with him when we get back from getting rid of the Fed. Then we're going to find out what kind of trick this guy just pulled."

The men dragged him back to the boiler room. Cole was too dazed to fight back. He felt himself landing hard on the warm cement floor, and then he heard the door slam shut and the turn of the key. The sound of their footsteps quickly faded away.

Cole was left alone in the hot room with the noisy boiler, and no way out.

Chug-chug-chug....

25

Cole tried the door, but of course that was of no use. It was too bad he didn't have his old lockpicks he once carried.

Next, he surveyed the boiler room, which was a space of about twenty by twenty feet. The ancient steampunk-style boiler took up a third. Besides the chair and the discarded ropes that had been used to tie up Michael Fuller, a small table stood against the back wall, upon which appeared to be some tools. Cole went to it and took stock. A crowbar, hammer, screwdriver…and that was it.

Those jerks were sure careless to leave these.

He picked up the screwdriver, went to the door, got on his knees, and attempted to use it in the keyhole. The flathead fit inside, but it wouldn't turn and couldn't be manipulated well enough to act as a pick. Cole fiddled with it for several minutes but eventually admitted it was futile.

He tried the crowbar next. The hinges on the metal door were made of iron. He tried to pry them off the concrete wall, but they wouldn't budge. He banged on them, kicked the door, cursed aloud, and finally threw the iron bar across the room.

It was damned warm in the boiler room. The thing was heating the entire hotel, so it had to be a powerful machine. Cole went closer to it and examined the pipes that went into the ceiling. He shook his head in frustration, for even if he did manage to break the exhaust away from the plaster, the hole and duct would not be big enough for him to crawl through. Besides, the boiler was *hot*. How would he climb up there without searing his skin? He might be dead, but he didn't relish feeling a burning sensation, even if it was only temporary and wouldn't do lasting damage.

Cole went back to the door, got on his knees again, and looked through the keyhole. He could barely make out the corridor beyond that led to the storage and laundry areas. He would just have to wait until Chadwick and his bozos returned. He'd surprise them with the crowbar, fight them, and maybe even win. How many times could they shoot him? A zillion, and he'd still be able to get up. Nevertheless, he wanted to avoid it.

"Have you looked for a portal?"

The female voice startled him. He let out a yelp and turned, falling on his butt.

Agnieszka was standing near the boiler.

"My God," Cole said. "Geez, you scared me. Agnieszka! How did you get in here? You can go through walls and stuff, but I can't?"

"I just told you there may be a portal in here." She gave him a smile and shrugged.

He got to his feet. "Where is it?"

As was her style, she didn't answer him. "What have you learned on your journeys through the past, Mr. Sackler?" she asked instead, crossing her arms like a schoolteacher.

The woman was still dressed as the gypsy fortune teller; but now that she was standing and not behind her little table, Cole could see once again that she had a lovely figure underneath that garb. "Uh, well, I now know who my real parents were, and that a gangster killed my father. If this is still 1948—I can never be sure about *when* I am—then I figure that my mother will die a little later this year in the fire that will break out in Room 302. My brother and I received our burn scars from that incident. Somehow, we survived, became wards of the state, and were then taken anonymously to an adoption agency in Queens. That's where I was adopted by the Sacklers. Am I right?"

"What do *you* think?"

"I think I am. Is there more I need to find out? When does this end?"

"You're getting closer to the truth. Tell me, Mr. Sackler, do you know what happened in this very room?"

"One of the hotel maids was murdered here, two years

before I came to work at the hotel. That was you, Agnieszka. Is that what you're referring to?"

"Perhaps."

"I've asked you before. Do you know who killed you? Because the police think it's the same person who shot all the murder victims in the hotel, starting with you."

"Maybe it was Charlie," she said.

He had suspected that, but finally hearing it from her lips disturbed him a great deal. He slammed his right fist into the palm of his left hand. "I knew it." He started to pace back and forth in the small space. "I knew he was the murderer. Where is he? He's alive and well, isn't he? He'd been stalking me when *I* was alive. I know it. When I see him in my memories, that's all he is, right? When I talk to him, *he's not really there*! I don't know how or why I've had that kind of connection to him all my life, but now I know he's *real* because he killed me! Where is he? *Where is he?*"

"He is closer than you think. First you need to find your way out of here."

"And you're not going to help me with that, are you?" Cole went to the wall to the right of the door and started moving his hands up and down, patting it, feeling the texture of the plaster, and searching for an opening. He made it to the corner and continued around to the adjoining wall. "Am I getting warmer? Huh? Agnieszka?"

He turned back to her and saw that she wasn't there.

Gone. Vanished.

"Aw, hell."

Cole felt exhausted and depressed. The scuffle with the mobsters had taken a lot out of him. All the running around and time-hopping and going through emotional discoveries—it was all sucking away his energy.

He dropped to the floor and sat Indian style. He closed his eyes and took deep breaths.

I wish I had a drink.

And then he drifted off into his memories…

…and the time he came home drunk on Christmas Eve 1980. He found Janine in a fancy dress, sitting at the kitchen table in their Brooklyn apartment, an empty glass and an empty bottle of champagne in front of her. Her head was on the table and she was out of it.

Ohhhh, shit. I forgot about our date. Goddamn it!

"Janine?" He stumbled to her and touched her on the shoulder. "Hey. Janine. Sorry, I got held up at the hotel...I got... Janine?"

She stirred, groaned, and opened her eyes. "You bastard," she mumbled, slurring her words. "You fucking bastard. Look... what you made me do."

"You drank that whole bottle?"

"You see anyone else in here?" She managed to raise her head. Janine's eyes were red.

Cole sat in the other chair.

He had met Janine Blakely at an AA meeting. She was a social worker, three years younger than he, with brown hair, a nice figure, and a cynical world outlook that matched his own. They were made for each other. Cole had decided to try AA after the Cindy Walker murder in the hotel in 1978. His first meeting was in early '79, and that's where he got to chatting with Janine. Apparently, she had a drinking problem, too, but she had been sober for four years. After a first, and then a second and third date, they were officially a couple. Cole had done his best to stay off the booze, although he slipped every two or three weeks. Janine understood and was tolerant of his predicament—at first. They were married in December of '79, found and rented an apartment near the R subway line in Brooklyn, and lived happily, sort of, for a while. No Dream States. No talking to Charlie. Cole commuted to the hotel every day, but his nighttime shifts were hard on the couple. Janine worked during the day, so they saw each other only for a couple of hours in the morning and evening. They almost never had meals together. Cole continued to struggle with the alcohol, and finally Janine read him the riot act. Again, he attempted to stop drinking. Janine found out she was pregnant in the spring of 1980, but she lost the baby five months in. That was a turning point for her, and then *she* fell off the wagon. By the end of the year, they were two sots in a cage. The fights became legendary. There was talk of divorce.

Then, a truce was made with the promise of an effort to get sober again and celebrate Christmas Eve together, but Cole had blown it.

"I'm sorry, Janine," he said quietly.

"What?"

"I said, 'I'm sorry!'"

"Screw you, Cole. Look at me. I was so upset…I drank again. It's your fault!"

"I didn't make you drink a bottle of champagne, Janine. I wasn't here."

"Exactly!" She closed her eyes and started to cry again. "Where *were* you?"

"At the hotel. I had to be…at our holiday party."

"You've been drinking, too."

"Yeah."

"You just wanted the free booze."

That was true. "Yeah."

"You're a liar, Cole. You don't have holiday parties at that fleabag hotel. Get out of here, Cole. Go back to the hotel and stay there tonight. I may not be here tomorrow, but I need to sleep this off. That divorce we talked about? It's on."

Cole simply nodded. He stood, picked up her empty glass, and threw it against the wall. It shattered into a dozen pieces, just like their marriage. He walked out and made his way back to Hotel Destiny, where he would live until he died.

The divorce was final in late 1981. Janine stayed in the apartment, but they didn't communicate or see each other again after they signed the papers. He'd heard she had found someone new…

…"Good job, Cole," came the male voice that jarred him out of his Dream State.

Cole opened his eyes. He was still sitting on the boiler room floor.

He looked up to see the man in the black cloak and white mask standing in front of the boiler.

26

"What did you say?" Cole asked.

"I said, you did a great job with your marriage. You managed to turn two recovering drunks back into, well, drunks. Bravo."

"Fuck you, Charlie."

Cole closed his eyes and rubbed his brow with his fingers.

I'm seeing things. He's not really here.

He looked up again, but Charlie was, sure enough, still there.

"How the hell did *you* get in here?" Cole asked.

"Do you remember when we used to play with toy army figures on the floor of your room and you always cheated?"

"What?"

"I'd say, 'My men are safely protected by these big rocks and trees,' or whatever obstacles I'd made up out of Lincoln Logs or other toys you had. Then you'd arbitrarily blow up the obstacles with a cannon you didn't really have, and then you'd kill my men with a fake explosion. You cheated."

This angered Cole. He got up off the floor and moved toward his twin. "Take off that mask."

"Oh, is Coley-Poley getting mad?"

"Don't call me that. Take off the mask. I want to see your face!"

"Not going to do it."

"Take it off!"

"Make me."

That did it. Cole jumped at the man and was surprised that he could feel and touch him. He reached for the white mask, but Charlie slammed both palms into Cole's chest, knocking him back. This further enraged Cole, so he leaped forward, tackled his twin brother, and knocked him against the hot boiler. They struggled as Cole attempted to reach for the mask, but Charlie was strong. He grasped both of Cole's arms and held them back. The two men were evenly matched, duplicates in size and strength.

Cole jerked his knee up hard into Charlie's groin, causing the other man to react in pain. The pressure against Cole's arms abated enough for him to finally shoot a hand to his brother's face and take hold of the mask. He ripped it away to reveal a mirror image of himself—except that the upper half of the face that had been covered by the disguise was horribly disfigured from severe burn scars. The skin was pink and waxy. There were no eyebrows. The area around the eyes were practically skeletal, and at first Cole thought that portions of the man's skull was poking through. Blue and red lines—veins?—that resembled bolts of thin lightning stood out on the forehead. The cloak hood dropped back to reveal a bald, terribly pock-marked cranium.

"Aggh!" Repulsed, Cole let go and retreated, taking several steps away from the hideous thing in front of him.

Charlie quickly recovered from the knee-jab and chuckled. "Yeah, I'm your twin! Aren't I pretty?" He then turned and opened the boiler's hatch, which was half the size of a standard door. Inside was a chamber large enough to climb into, but it was full of flames. Charlie ducked, thrust his upper body into the boiler, and climbed all the way in. The hatch slammed shut...and he was gone.

Cole's jaw dropped.

What the hell *just happened?*

He went and opened the hatch and looked inside.

Nothing but a blazing fire.

Is this...is this the portal?

It made no sense, but Cole was beginning to think it was his only way out of the boiler room, unless he waited to confront Chadwick and his boys.

Remember—I'm already dead! The flames can't hurt me. Well, at first, maybe, but not for long.

"I can't possibly go in there," he said aloud.

He was deathly afraid of fire.

It won't kill me. I'm already dead.

He hesitated, and then he ducked low enough to get his head inside.

"Shit, shit, shit...."

He took the plunge.

Cole poked his head and shoulders into the boiler. The flames lapped at his face. He jumped up so that he could get the rest of his upper torso in.

Yes, he felt the burning.

His legs were off the floor. He crawled in, shut the hatch...

...and screamed in terror as the flames surrounded him.

27

The smoke made it difficult to breathe. Cole coughed and sputtered and waved his arms around to try and clear it. He came to the realization that he was no longer inside the boiler, but rather in a much larger space. A place with furniture, a window….

I'm in one of the hotel rooms!

He could barely make out through the flames the living room of one of the suites on the third floor. It looked vaguely familiar—a coffee table that was the focus of a sofa/comfy chair combination, an archway to the left that went to a kitchen. The way out was through a T-intersection corridor. One way went to bedrooms and the other to the front door of the apartment.

The Apartment. I'm in Room 302! This is the night the fire started in the suite!

He rushed for the door with his eyes closed, his hands outstretched—luckily, he knew the way. The door was open, which made his frantic exit easier. He burst into the third-floor hallway…

…and everything changed.

Suddenly there was no smoke or fire. The stillness was such a shock that he gasped loudly for air, moved to the wall in front of him, leaned on it with both arms bent at the elbows, and rested his forehead on one forearm. He felt the sweat on his body, so he straightened, undid the stupid bow tie and unbuttoned the tuxedo shirt. Even though the blaze was now a memory, it was obviously a hot summer day in the hotel.

That's when he heard a woman crying out in agony behind him.

He turned and saw that the door to Room 302 was closed.

The wail had come from inside. Curly Chadwick and Shake were right beside him in the hallway. Chadwick was pacing, a few feet toward the end of the corridor, and then a few feet the other direction to the elevators. Back and forth. The two men couldn't see or hear Cole.

"Boss, maybe you should sit down somewhere and try to relax," Shake said.

Chadwick stopped and gave his underling the bug-eye. "Relax? You want me to *relax*?" Chadwick pulled back a fist, ready to strike his loyal henchman, who quickly put up his hands.

"Boss, wait, hey, it's me! I'm just trying to help. You seem... tense."

Chadwick pointed to the door. "Tense? I seem tense? Miranda's having a baby in there! And the kid *ain't mine!*"

"Come on, boss, you don't know that for sure...."

"I don't? You contradicting me?"

"No, boss, I—"

"Then *shut up!*"

Another howl from inside the apartment. Cole could hear a second voice, a woman encouraging Miranda, saying things like, "Almost there" and "Push" and "You can do it!"

Cole flattened his back against the wall, facing the door.

My God...I'm being born in there...!

In the weird and surreal way that the metaphysics worked in the ghost world, he had gone through a portal inside the boiler in the basement, passed through the night in 1948 when the possible arson had occurred, and then ended up here, earlier, on the afternoon of his birth. What day was it? Did it matter?

Shake mumbled, "Jesus, she's been in labor a long time."

Another scream. Chadwick put his hands to his ears. "I can't stand it! It's horrible!"

And then there was the miraculous sound of a baby crying.

Shake grabbed Chadwick's huge upper arm. "Boss! Listen!"

The man did so and made a face.

Miranda yelped again, followed by more enthusiastic coaching from the woman who was with her. The baby continued to let the world know it did not like this strange new environment, but Cole recognized two different pitches in the streaming cacophony of newborns crying. He knew there were two of them.

A few minutes passed, and the noise died down. The baby— babies?—were settling down. Chadwick started to walk away toward the elevators. "I'm going downstairs."

The door to 302 opened.

"Boss! Wait!"

Chadwick stopped and turned.

A woman in her forties and dressed in a nurse's uniform emerged, saw Chadwick, and approached him. Her apron was messy and bloody.

"Congratulations, Mr. Chadwick," she said, "you are the father of two healthy boys! Twins!"

"*Twins?*" he shouted with his hands over his chest, as if he were having a heart attack.

"Isn't it wonderful?"

Chadwick looked as if he might faint. He took a step backwards, collected himself, and quickly regained composure. "Uh, thank you, Nurse Abigail. How is Miranda?"

"Tired and weak, but she's fine. I better get back inside."

"Sure, I'll be in soon."

Abigail returned to the apartment, but she left the door open.

"How about that, boss?" Shake blurted. "Twins!"

"Miranda said once she thought she might be having twins. She wouldn't tell me why she thought that. No doctor has ever seen her."

"You'll have to give away *two* cigars to everybody now!"

"Shake—*shut up!*"

Cole stared at the open door. It beckoned to him.

Why not? While I'm invisible….

He moved forward and re-entered the suite without the gangsters knowing. He stopped in the entryway, concerned about the portal that was somewhere in Room 302. After all, he'd just passed through it when it was on fire and ended up sometime earlier. Would it happen again? He moved slowly, came to the T-intersection, and waited. The master bedroom door down the hall to his left was open. Nothing changed, so he made his way there. He hesitantly peeked inside and saw Abigail tending to soiled towels and basins of water. Miranda lay in the bed, a look of exhausted contentment on her face. Her eyes were closed, her mouth slightly open. Her right arm was wrapped around a swaddled child whose head lay on her breast. The left arm duplicated the picture with a second infant. Cole didn't know which one was him, for both babies looked exactly the same.

Abigail left the room carrying the towels, and Cole was alone with his mother and her children.

Miranda opened her eyes, and they slightly widened, focusing on him.

"You." She was too weak to be upset to see the ghost standing in front of her.

"Hello," Cole said. "Congratulations."

"Have you...have you come to take my sons?"

"Not at all. You should rest, Miranda."

A full minute passed in silence.

"I'm going to end it," she finally said.

Cole's brow creased. "What do you mean?"

"I can't live with this. With them. With *him*."

"Curly?"

Then she asked, "Why...why have you been...haunting me?"

"Because one of those babies is me."

She closed her eyes and wrinkled her brow. "Wha—what?"

Cole grimaced. It was something he shouldn't have said. "Never mind. Just rest. I'm leaving."

He turned to go and ran into Abigail, who had just returned.

"Who are you?" she asked, startled.

"A friend. I'm just going. Excuse me." He pushed past her, moved into the hallway, and headed for the Apartment door.

"Mr. Chadwick!" the midwife called. "Mr. Chadwick!"

Cole didn't look back. He strode toward the elevators as, behind him, Chadwick shouted, "Hey, you!"

Cole ran for the Grand Stairs, but one of the elevator indicator lights *dinged* and its doors opened. Cole rushed in, turned, and saw Chadwick and Shake barreling toward him. Cole pushed the number "1" and then the "Close Doors button," jabbing it repeatedly, urging the machinery to hurry up. Finally, the doors shut, just as Chadwick reached them.

The elevator didn't move.

Come on…!

He pressed the "1" button again.

Nothing happened, until he perceived the shift in lighting and felt the floor of the car tremble…

…The doors opened automatically.

It was night in the hotel. Cole immediately knew it by instinct, and there was also a room service tray on the floor outside Room 301, which hadn't been there before. This was a different day and time.

Just ahead, Curly Chadwick was struggling with Shake and two of his men in the hallway right in front of Room 302, the door to which was open.

"Boss, put it down! Don't do it!" Shake pleaded.

"Let go of me! I can't stand it anymore!"

A burning Molotov cocktail—a Coke bottle filled with gasoline and a flaming rag sticking out of the neck—was in Chadwick's right hand. It appeared that he was trying to throw it into the apartment.

"You're crazy, boss! Stop it!"

BANG!

Shake jolted and let go of the big man, stumbled backwards, and clutched his belly. Cole could now see that Chadwick held a pistol in his left hand.

"Boss! You…shot me!"

BANG!

Shake fell in the hallway and said nothing else.

"And I shot you again," Chadwick said.

The two other goons immediately held up their hands and backed away. Chadwick aimed the gun at them as the flame on the cocktail's rag snaked dangerously close to the liquid in the bottle. The men turned and ran the opposite direction toward the fire escape stairs.

Cole stood frozen in place, too stunned to move.

Curly Chadwick tossed the Molotov cocktail into the room, where it exploded with percussive force.

28

The fireball burst into the hallway. Chadwick was driven back to the corridor wall, watching his handiwork with a mixture of fascination and horror. He dropped his handgun and fell to his knees, and then he buried his face in his hands.

"God forgive me!" he shouted.

Cole leapt into action by bolting out of the elevator and running toward the suite. Other men and Abigail, the nurse, had also appeared. She shrieked in terror, hysterically babbling that the babies were inside with Miranda. The gangsters attempted to enter the room, but they were overcome by the smoke and flames and couldn't move more than ten feet into the apartment.

There were shouts of "Call the fire department!" and "Where are the extinguishers?"

Cole maneuvered past the cowering group that was attempting to pull Chadwick off the floor and get him to move, and then stood in the suite doorway. The flames had overtaken the T-intersection hallway and the living room was ablaze. However, the corridor to the bedrooms had not been engulfed too badly yet.

He rushed in, battling the heat and the blaze, made a left turn, and hurried to the master bedroom.

Miranda's position was grossly unnatural. The top half of her body was hanging off the bed, and her arms hung loosely to the floor. A pistol lay by her right hand. Cole then saw that the blonde hair on one side of her head was matted with a deeply red, viscous liquid.

"No!" Cole cried aloud. "NO!"

He started to go to her, but then he realized that the two newborns were not in the room.

They must come first!

Cole turned and darted back into the hallway, where the flames were now encroaching with increasing intensity. The nursery—where the two cribs were—was just two doors away. He skirted through the burning torture and stepped inside to see that the fire had already covered half of the room. The cribs themselves were ablaze and the babies were screaming their heads off.

Laurence and Theresa Flynn stood between the cribs. The expressions on their faces indicated that they were desperate for help.

"Let's get those kids out of here!" Cole yelled.

The Flynns nodded. Laurence turned to one crib and Theresa to the other. They each picked up one of the babies, who were wrapped in blankets that were smoldering. The two ghosts did their best to pat and beat the embers away.

"Give them to me!" Cole held out his arms.

Theresa placed one of the boys into the cradle of his bent right arm, and then Laurence settled the other child in Cole's left. Cole held both babies tightly, turned, and headed out of the room. The fire in the hallway was now a maelstrom. It scared the hell out of him, and this caused him to hesitate.

Cole glanced back into the nursery. The Flynns had vanished. Maybe they had never been there. He would never know.

There was only one way out, and that was to carry the twins through the flames.

I can't be hurt! I'm already dead!

After reminding himself again of that macabre truth, he ducked his head and moved forward. He built up speed and plowed through the inferno until he reached the intersection. He hung a quick right and then shot out the door and into the hallway.

"Look!"

"Who's that?"

"He's got the babies!"

Chadwick was being held back by his men, but his size and bulk was too much for them. He suddenly broke free and rushed at the door. "Miranda!" he yelled as he moved past Cole and speared headlong into the firestorm. Mere seconds later, there was a horrible crash in the apartment as a flaring section of its ceiling caved in.

Better late than never, firefighters arrived at the top of the Grand Stairs by the elevators. They carried extinguishers and other equipment, shouting for all the onlookers to get the hell out of the building. "Evacuate! Evacuate! Take the stairs! The stairs!"

Cole kept moving toward the end of the hallway. He spotted Abigail at the top of the stairs, watching the disaster from a relatively safe vantage. Her eyes were full of tears and she hugged herself in despondency.

"Nurse!"

Her eyes focused on him and her jaw dropped. The sight of him holding the twins was an inexplicable miracle.

He approached her. "Take them! Please!"

Abigail nodded and held out her hands. Cole gently placed both crying babies in her arms.

"Get them to an ambulance! Hurry, they've been burned!"

At first, she just stood there, somewhat in shock.

"GO!"

Then the nurse turned and moved quickly down the stairs.

Cole went back into the third-floor hallway to watch as the firefighters attempted to enter the suite. The flames were now immense. There was no way that Curly Chadwick could have survived inside.

When more firemen poured onto the floor from the stairs, he knew that there was nothing more he could do. Cole descended the staircase all the way to the hotel lobby. He watched as the employees, gangsters, and guests flowed out into the street through the front doors. Three fire trucks were in place, and one firefighter directed foot traffic.

Stepping outside would be impossible. Instead, Cole made his way to the reception desk, pulled up the section of counter and opened the gate, and went straight to the sanctuary that would one day be his office. Even in 1948, the little room looked the same. After all, the desk he'd used as night manager and hotel detective had been a decades-old antique.

He shut the door, moved behind the desk, and sat.

Was that what really happened?

His mother had shot herself. Curly Chadwick, in a crazed moment of guilt and jealousy and hatred, had attempted to "erase" what she had done and eliminate the two souls she had produced without him.

And then that begged the question....

Did I, a ghost from the future, really save my own life—and my brother's—on that fateful day?

Tears ran down his face.

It was the only good thing he'd ever done, and he'd accomplished it only after he was dead.

Was this the heritage that Agnieszka had mentioned? Had he finished the journey by learning the truth about his parents and his birth?

No. Something is still missing.

That realization forced him to close his eyes and, unwittingly, Cole entered a final, revealing Dream State...

29

...**and** he got off the bus from New Jersey. Dressed in his army uniform, he threw his duffel bag over his shoulder and carried it with one strong arm as he made his way out of the scuzzy Port Authority building. His time in Vietnam had been a glimpse of hell, and yet seeing Manhattan again reminded him of how much of a cesspool it was, too, especially in this area of town near Times Square.

The year—1970.

He remembered this scene vividly. Cole Sackler, age twenty-two, crossed Eighth Avenue and walked east on 42nd Street. He'd had no idea where he was going to go. There was a medical discharge from the army after a harrowing few months in a Saigon hospital, and the repercussions of it played havoc on his psyche. They'd told him he'd had a "breakdown," and there wasn't much about it that he recalled. Something to do with fire in the jungle.

He supposed he should call his parents. Would Fred and Florence Sackler be happy to see him? Or would his "problems" in the army be a stigma to them?

When Cole reached Broadway and 42nd Street, he found that he was no longer carrying the duffel bag or dressed in his army uniform. Now he wore a cheap suit and carried a camera. It felt like late afternoon outside, a brisk day between winter and spring. For a moment, he was confused and disoriented, but then he recognized his old boss, the alcoholic private investigator—a guy named Milton Troy—standing at the corner, waiting for him.

The time had shifted to a couple of years later. Now it was 1972, and Cole had been back in the U.S. for a year and a half. He'd had a rough time of it. Menial jobs, a crappy studio apartment in SoHo, estrangement from his adoptive parents, and too much booze. The new job as the P.I.'s assistant was fairly interesting, though, but Milton Troy was a bad influence. There was always whiskey available at the seedy office on Eighth Avenue, and Cole's assignments often took him to sleazy spots that were so disgusting that alcohol was the only crutch that saw him through the work.

While the theatre district for many years had its share of "adult entertainment" tourist traps, the early seventies was the beginning of the huge boom in the porn industry. It was the year of *Deep Throat*. Various organized crime rivalries were taking over storefronts to create the peep show and adult bookstore businesses, movie houses were running X-rated fare, and pimps and their stables of "merchandise" were all over the streets. Drug dealers were blatant in the hawking of "smoke, uppers, downers, horse, coke," and any number of other temptations.

Luckily for me, all I need to do is walk into a liquor store to get what I need.

"There you are," Troy said. "You're late."

"I am?"

Troy pointed to his watch. "I pay you to be on time. Are you drunk again?"

"Jesus, Milton, usually I'm waiting on *you*. Speak for yourself. What's up?"

"I need you to get a room at the Hotel Destiny, just down the block off Seventh Avenue. A client hired us to get photographic evidence of her cheating husband. Apparently, he regularly meets up with a hooker named Lulu on the twelfth floor, Room 1208. You need to ask for Room 1207, right across the hall, and stay there until you hear activity going on. After that, well, you know what to do." Troy handed Cole a photograph of a middle-aged man who looked like he might be a Wall Street type. "That's him."

Cole stuck the photo in his jacket pocket, brushing against the Smith & Wesson he carried in a shoulder holster. He had managed to buy the weapon after his army discharge. Now the gun was a part of him, almost another appendage.

"How long do I have to be in the hotel?"

"As long as it takes. The guy sees Lulu twice a week, but it's unpredictable."

"Gotcha."

Cole took off east to Seventh and then headed south to where Hotel Destiny stood on the corner of one of the cross streets. He had known the fleabag joint had been there forever, that it was a place for transients and bums and crime, and that it wasn't particularly safe.

Wait a minute. I don't remember this at all. Is this one of my memories?

He eventually reached the front doors of the hotel. A homeless bum sat on the sidewalk against the wall, a pint of something inside a paper bag in his hand. "Spare change?" the man asked. Cole ignored him.

When he walked into the lobby, Cole thought he'd been in latrines that smelled better. A tall, thin man who looked like a gangster movie extra appeared behind the reception desk when Cole slapped the bell on the counter.

"Yes, sir?"

"I'd like a room, please. Twelfth floor. Is Room 1207 available?"

The employee raised his eyebrows at the specific request. He turned to check the row of mail slots and dangling room keys. He grabbed one and slapped it on the counter. "Room 1207. How many nights are you staying, sir?"

"I don't know yet."

"Pay in cash only, please, forty-five dollars. Check out is noon unless you pay for the next night before then."

"That's highway robbery for a dump like this."

"Take it or leave it. You're two blocks from Times Square."

Cole paid the man and asked for a receipt so he could be reimbursed. He then walked across the trashy lobby and noted the decaying antique furniture that had probably been there for decades.

Why don't I remember doing this? Was I really in Hotel Destiny on an assignment two years before I got hired to be the night manager and hotel detective?

He rang for the elevator—one of them was "out of service." He waited...and waited...and finally it arrived. The faded-gold doors opened. A shifty-looking guy wearing a purple zoot suit stood inside. Classic pimp costume. He didn't exit.

"I'm going up," Cole said.

"So am I," the pimp replied.

Okay. Cole stepped inside and pressed the number "12." The doors took an eternity to close and then the lift slowly rose. There was silence for a few awkward moments, and then the pimp removed a switchblade, flicked it open, and pointed it at Cole.

"Your wallet," the man growled.

Cole deftly reached into his jacket. "Sure, one second." He retrieved the Smith & Wesson, pulled it out, and pointed the barrel at the guy's nose. "Your face."

"Okay, man, okay." The guy closed the knife and put it back into his pocket. "You win." The man pushed the next floor's button, which was "6." The elevator stopped, the doors opened, and he got out in a hurry.

When the doors closed, Cole returned the gun to its holster and muttered, "Punk."

Did that really happen back in 1972?

He finally reached the twelfth floor, got out, and walked down the corridor. Sure enough, 1207 was directly across from 1208. Cole put his ear to the door of the latter and heard a woman laughing, followed by a man howling, "Yeah, that's it, woof woof woof! I'm the Big Bad Woof!" Cole shook his head—it took all types—and then used the key on his own door.

It was a typical no-frills room. A queen-size bed, a bathroom, table and two chairs, a closet, and a small dresser. A couple of lamps, one with a burned-out bulb when he tried them. The window looked out at the back of a taller building, so the view was nothing but bricks. The bathroom was clean, but there appeared to be mold in the corners of the tile floor. At least there was toilet paper in the dispenser.

Cole removed a pint of Jack Daniel's from his jacket pocket, took off the jacket, and sat in one of the chairs. He began to nurse the booze and contemplate the meaninglessness of his current existence. As for his assignment, he couldn't care less about Mr. Wall Street and Lulu. He could always say that the guy never showed up, and Cole would still get a minimum salary...

...The next thing he knew, the room was dark and the bottle nearly empty. Had he fallen asleep? He heard what sounded like a noisy vacuum cleaner in the hallway. After a few minutes, it started to annoy him, so he got up, put his jacket on over the gun and holster, went to the door, and opened it.

A pretty young woman wearing a maid uniform was indeed vacuuming.

"Excuse me," he said.

She looked up. Dark hair, brown eyes, a nice figure. "Yes, sir?" She had an undefinable European accent.

"What time is it?"

She looked at a watch on her wrist. "Almost six."

"In the morning?"

"Yes, sir."

"And you're vacuuming?"

"I am sorry, sir. Was it too loud? Did I disturb you?"

"I suspect you're disturbing everyone."

"You're the only one on the floor, sir. I am sorry. I wanted to get off work early and finish. My apologies."

Cole looked up and down the hallway. He pointed at 1208. "There's no one in there?"

"She checked out, sir."

"Hm. Okay."

"I am just leaving now. Sorry to disturb you."

She turned and rolled the vacuum toward the elevators. She pushed the "Down" button and waited.

Cole closed the door behind him and hurried to catch it before the lift arrived. When the doors opened, he was standing beside her. "I'll go down with you, if you don't mind."

"No, sir, it's all right."

She pressed the "B" button. Cole pressed the "1."

"What's in the basement?" he asked.

The doors closed and the elevator began to move.

"The laundry, storage, the boiler, and loading ramp to street."

Cole eyed the plastic name tag pinned to her blouse. AGNIESZKA.

My God. Did I meet Agnieszka in 1972? WHY DON'T I REMEMBER THIS?

"Are you from Poland?" he asked.

"Yes, sir."

She was enchantingly beautiful. Cole wondered if he should ask for a phone number. Instead, he said, "Well, welcome to the land of opportunity."

That made her laugh a little. "In Poland I was a fortune teller."

"Really? A fortune teller? Like a *gypsy* fortune teller?"

That classification didn't seem to amuse her. "No, just a fortune teller."

The elevator stopped at the first floor and the doors opened. That shook Cole out of the spell she'd cast on him, and then he said, "Well, have a good day."

"You, too, sir."

He stepped out, but another man, the same height and shape as he, moved past him and entered the car with Agnieszka. Cole turned to look at him, puzzled as hell.

The man was dressed in a tuxedo, a black cloak and hood, and was wearing a white mask.

The doors closed and the lift went down to the basement. He shut his eyes and rubbed them.

Charlie. That was Charlie!...

...Cole opened his eyes again to see that he was staring at himself. The jolt made him gasp, and then he realized he was looking at the mirror on the wall of his old office in the hotel. He turned and surveyed the room. The desk, chair, lamps, and the door to his little bedroom that he had fashioned out of the adjoining office...this was exactly the way it was when he'd been *shot* by his murderous twin.

He'd come out of the Dream State and now here he was. He had no recollection of that night in 1972. He didn't remember the P.I. assignment there, or meeting Agnieszka Preisner in the elevator. Had he really been there? Had he been in Hotel Destiny prior to his employment?

And what about Charlie? He *saw* him! His brother got in the elevator with Agnieszka, and it was going down to the *basement*. Where the boiler room was located.

Agnieszka was shot and killed in the boiler room. In 1972!

That's why he re-lived the moment—so that he would remember it and then know what he had to do!

He went over to the desk and saw the newspaper laying there—the *New York Daily Herald*, dated October 31, 1985. It was open to the article about Hotel Destiny's grand re-opening and Halloween costume gala.

Cole looked at the clock...not yet 10:00 p.m.

This *is my heritage, then! I'm back where I started, and I can stop my serial killer twin from killing more people!*

He opened the desk drawer and grabbed the faithful Smith & Wesson that was there. He then went to the closet and found the black cloak and white mask he had planned to wear to the Halloween party as the hotel detective in disguise. He put on the cloak and mask, stuck the gun in his pocket, and left the office.

This time he didn't greet Virginia or Carolyn at the front desk. He moved across the lobby and around the arriving guests and security men, and then he bounded with a purpose up the Grand Stairs.

30

The gala was in full swing in the Grand Room. It was just as he remembered it on the night he'd died. The color scheme was black and white with splashes of blood-red, mostly in the tablecloths covering the highboys where guests could stand, converse, and enjoy their cocktails. The large square checkerboard dance floor was lit by the magnificent chandelier that hung overhead. Other fixtures threw splashes of bright spots around the room to highlight areas of interest. The twelve-piece band was playing early jazz that was lively and danceable. A crooner sang numbers like "At the Darktown Strutter's Ball" and "For Me and My Gal." Hired women incongruously dressed as "flappers" carried trays of hoers d'oeuvres and complimentary champagne flutes. The crowd of guests grew by the minute. The costumes, of course, were not relegated to the 1917 era. There were witches, Ronald Reagans, Darth Vaders, princesses, sexy nurses, zombies, and the many men wearing identical tuxes, black cloaks with hoods, and white masks.

Mounted on the opposite wall from the bar were the two restored, ten-foot-tall paintings of Laurence Flynn and wife, Theresa. Standing beneath them, watching Cole's every move, were the ghosts of Laurence and Theresa themselves. Their expressions were expectant, as if something were about to happen.

Cole nodded to them, and then circulated through the crowd. Could he be seen and heard? He didn't know and didn't care. Probably best to be invisible. He had no desire to converse with anyone.

He spotted Marvin Trent, the new owner, standing with his wife and conversing with New York VIPs. And there—on the dance floor—was his floozy daughter, Louise. As before, she was dressed as Little Bo Peep. Her partner was a man *also* wearing a black cloak and white mask.

Cole continued to circle the space. When he came back around to the paintings, he found none other than Agnieszka, dressed as the gypsy fortune teller, sitting at her little table. FREE PALM READINGS.

"I'm about to finish my journey," he said to her.

She looked at him with those seductive, knowing eyes. "I think you might be right."

"Charlie killed you in the boiler room. I'm going to stop him from killing others."

"He is here, Mr. Sackler. Your twin is in the room."

"Where?"

"Find him!"

She looked down, ending the conversation the way she always did.

Cole stepped away and surveyed the dance floor. Now he couldn't find Louise. Had she been dancing with *Charlie*? Where did she go? Where did *he* go? Determined to end this crazy thing, Cole thought he would confront every fellow in the place who was dressed in a cloak and mask. One man costumed as such was at the bar, so Cole approached him and started to pull out the gun from his pocket. The man turned and revealed the lower half of his face, which was covered with a beard and mustache. He wasn't Charlie.

Damn it.

From there, Cole hurried to the ballroom doors and peered into the foyer.

THERE!

The man in the cloak and white mask who had been watching *him* on the night of the gala before he was murdered was standing at the top of the staircase.

Charlie.

"Hey!" Cole shouted, but the man, not hearing him, began to descend to the first floor. Cole set off after him, but a group of women stepped in front of him on their way out of the bathroom. They inexplicably halted, blocking his way as they gabbed and chattered.

"Excuse me, ladies!" he barked, but they ignored him. Cole started to go around them, but they finally went on back into the ballroom. He rushed to the staircase, rapidly took the steps two at a time, and reached the lobby.

He glimpsed his prey disappearing behind the reception desk, moving toward the administrative offices.

Cole ran across the space, zig zagging between guests. He paid no attention to Victoria and Carolyn, pulled up the counter section, opened the gate, and stepped into the hallway leading to his office. His brother had left the door open.

Cole removed the Smith & Wesson from his jacket pocket. Striding resolutely, he held the gun out in front of him and entered the room he had come to know so well during his employment as the night manager and hotel detective.

Charlie was standing at the mirror, looking at his masked reflection, straightening his bow tie, and singing to himself, "Has any-bod-y seen my gal…?"

Cole swiftly moved closer and raised the gun. In the mirror image, he saw Charlie's eyes meet his own and widen with surprise.

BANG!

Charlie's brains and blood and gore splattered the glass. The man sagged and dropped to the faded carpet. A pool of blood briskly formed around the twin's head.

Cole felt an immense sensation of satisfaction. He wanted to jump for joy. After stuffing the weapon back into his pocket, he stood over the body, bent down, and pulled up the white mask.

The dead man's face was his own. No burn scars. No sign that he had ever been in a fire.

Cole gasped aloud, let go of the mask, and tumbled backwards in horror.

What have I done? MY GOD, WHAT HAVE I DONE?

He heard a woman laughing behind him. There, in the doorway, stood Agnieszka. She was no longer wearing the gypsy fortune teller costume but was instead dressed as a hotel maid.

"What just happened?" he asked, his entire body trembling with fear.

"You killed yourself, Coleman Sackler," she answered.

"But...he was Charlie!"

"Look again. The man on the floor is you. Charlie, your twin brother, died as a newborn in that fire in Room 302, in 1948."

Cole began to hyperventilate. "What are you talking about?"

She made a *tsk tsk* sound. "When you visited your memories, your *Dream States*, as you call them, your mind simply refused to hear or see portions of those events. You've been in denial your entire life."

What?...

...Cole was suddenly back on the floor of his room, five years old, playing with his dinosaur toys.

"Cole?" came a woman's voice. "Who are you talking to?"

The little boy looked up and saw his adoptive mother standing in the open doorway.

Florence Sackler.

"Charlie," he answered out of little Cole's mouth.

"Charlie? Again?" his mother put a hand on her hip. "Honey, what's your imaginary friend saying to you this time?"

"His tyr-an-no-saurus will eat my bront-o-saurus!"

Cole looked at where Charlie had been moments before, but he wasn't there. Cole was alone in his room.

"Oh, well, don't let him do that." She looked around the space. "I want you to pick up your room, Cole. It's a mess. I'll come back in a little while and it had better be done, okay?"

"Okay."

"And...honey?" His mother made a sad face and shook her head. "I don't know what you remember about your brother, because you were just a baby. But Charlie didn't survive that fire. You've made up Charlie in your head." She then blinked, regretting what she had just said. "I'm sorry, darling. I didn't mean that. You just continue playing, all right?"

Cole watched his mother as she left the room...

...And then Dr. Patterson's voice brought Cole to another place and time. Just as abruptly as before, he was now lying on the therapist's couch back in 1967.

"You had been telling me how your parents discouraged

you from having an imaginary friend when you were a child," the doctor said.

"Oh. Right."

"You said you believed he was your twin brother?"

"Yeah. I mean, I knew I didn't have a twin brother. But I pretended I did."

"Why do you think you felt the need to invent a twin brother?"

"I don't know! I was five or six years old."

"But you just said a few minutes ago that you continue to talk to him when you're alone."

"I did?"

"Yes, Cole, you did. Something about 'Dream States'?"

When Cole didn't answer, Dr. Patterson said, "We've discussed this before. Your brother, Charlie, died when you were both newborns. His burns were too severe. The orphanage people explained that to your adoptive parents."

"*I didn't hear it that way!*" Cole shouted, rising to a sitting position. "I heard the administrator talk about Charlie's burns being more severe than mine, but she didn't say he'd died!"

The doctor wrinkled his brow. "How could you have heard that?"

The sweat ran down Cole's forehead. What was happening to him? Why was his reality taking a downward spiral into a nightmare?...

...Back in his hotel office in 1985, staring at Agnieszka, Cole stammered, "But...I saved the babies from the fire! As a ghost! Right? I carried them from my mother's bedroom out of Room 302 and gave them to Abigail, the nurse!"

Agnieszka sighed. "Even that act did not turn out as you think."

Cole started to protest...

...But then his mind went back to the third floor on the night of the fire in 1948. Flames, smoke, heat, people crying and yelling, and total chaos.

He carried the two infants from Miranda's bedroom, out into the hallway, and spotted Abigail. Her eyes were full of tears and she hugged herself in despondency.

"Nurse!"

Her eyes focused on him and her jaw dropped. The sight of him holding the twins was an inexplicable miracle.

He approached her. "Take them! Please!"

Abigail nodded and held out her hands. Cole gently placed both babies in her arms.

"Get them to an ambulance! Hurry, they've been burned!"

At first, she just stood there, somewhat in shock.

"GO!"

But then he could see that the nurse was studying them and professionally keeping her emotions in check. "Thank God one of them is still alive. Little Coleman. But...oh, poor Charles. I'm afraid...Charles is gone. What a tragedy." Abigail looked at him. "Thank you, though. You saved one of them."

Then the nurse turned and moved quickly down the stairs...

...The lighting shifted and Cole felt a tremor in the floor. He was back in his office, standing over his dead corpse, and speaking to Agnieszka.

"You refused to believe what really happened to your twin brother," she said. "It split your mind in two."

"You're lying!" Cole spat. "I went to the orphanage. I broke into the office and I saw the file. Charlie was adopted by a family named Whitten!"

"You imagined that. It was another part of your delusion that your brother was still alive. I'm no psychologist, but your trauma as a newborn infected your mind, divided it, and you've been very sick ever since. You're a murderer, Coleman Sackler. It wasn't Charlie who killed all those victims in the hotel—and me—it was you. Those Dream States of yours? They were blackouts in which your sick side, your *Charlie* side, took over."

Cole wanted to scream. "That's not true! It can't be!"

And then came the flashes of imagery—

His own hand holding a gun and shooting call-girl Martine Crawford in the head in Room 605.

His own hand holding a gun and shooting hotel guest Chantal Lee in the head in Room 907.

His own hand holding a gun and shooting drug addict Cindy Walker in the head in Room 1015.

His own hand holding a gun and shooting drug dealer Hutch Butler in the head in Room 711.

And his own hand holding a gun and shooting hotel maid Agnieszka Preisner in the head in the boiler room.

Cole dropped to his knees. He covered his face with his hands and began to sob.

He had also killed himself…

…Cole's fevered brain flashed back to when he was alive on Halloween night, 1985, as he stood in his office waiting for Louise to show up. He was staring into the mirror on the wall at his masked reflection.

"Has any-bod-y seen my gal?" he sang as he straightened his bow tie.

There was movement behind him in the reflection.

Someone had entered the office.

Ah, she's here already!

Still looking in the mirror, Cole watched the figure emerge from the shadows. He expected Little Bo Peep, but instead it was the man in the cloak and white mask.

Cole reflexively started to turn, but the man's approach was fast and catlike. A raised pistol pointed at his head, and it fired without warning.

There was no time for a scream. There was no time for anything, anymore. The journey through Hotel Destiny had been nothing but a tragic circle…

…Agnieszka's voice brought him back to him kneeling beside his own corpse. "My own task is completed," she said. "I can now leave this wretched place. You, however, must stay."

She turned and left the office.

Cole looked up. "Wait. Agnieszka!"

He bolted to his feet and ran after her. When he reached the lobby, he watched as she opened the doors and stepped out to the street. She stood on the sidewalk, looked up and raised her arms for a moment, and then she vanished.

Cole went to the door and opened it. Once again, the black, torrential winds blew him back into the building. There was no fighting it and there was no escape.

"No. No. No. I'm sorry. I'm sorry. I'm sorry." He cried and

beat on the glass doors until there was no energy left, nothing to give him any hope for a change.

After a few moments, Cole felt a presence behind him.

He turned around to see that they were all standing in the lobby, watching him. Faces he knew and faces he didn't. Well over a dozen figures. He did recognize Hutch Butler, Cindy Walker, Chantal Lee, and Martine Crawford. His victims gazed at him with hatred in their eyes.

Curly Chadwick towered behind the reception desk.

The actor, Bradley Granger, was on the staircase.

His grandparents, Laurence and Theresa Flynn, hovered nearby. Laurence held a pistol in his hand. He unlatched the cylinder, spun it, snapped it shut, pointed the barrel at his head, and squeezed the trigger.

Click.

Cole's birth mother, Miranda Flynn, stood with his real father, Michael Fuller, directly in front of him. She held a swaddled, perpetually crying baby in her arms, the blanket charred from being burned.

"Welcome, son," Miranda said. "Come meet your brother, Charlie."

Cole's resulting screams echoed through the many rooms, hallways, memories, and dreams that were permanent fixtures of Hotel Destiny.

FROM
THE NEW YORK DAILY HERALD
NOVEMBER 2, 1985

HOTEL DESTINY
RE-OPENING
MARRED BY TRAGEDY

After years of operating as a transient and often controversial landmark near Times Square in Manhattan, the twelve-story Hotel Destiny re-opened in grand style on Halloween night with a costume party attended by New York's mayor and other dignitaries and society page personalities.

New owner and manager Marvin Trent reported that the evening was a huge success and that he hopes the hotel will enjoy a long and prosperous business in the Times Square area.

Unfortunately, though, the celebratory evening was somewhat marred by the apparent suicide of longtime night manager and self-professed hotel detective, Coleman Sackler. Mr. Sackler's body was found in his office, a Smith & Wesson revolver lying next to his hand. According to the police, the weapon is suspected to be linked to past murders that have occurred in the building.

On that subject, Trent says, "Mr. Sackler worked

for the hotel for many years. I'm afraid his behavior and drinking problem was about to result in his termination in the next week anyway. It's sad and I'm sorry, but if the police are correct, then it's a good thing he's gone."

NYPD's Sergeant Redenius of the 14th Precinct gave a statement to the press. "I have personally known Mr. Sackler for years. He was an alcoholic and an anti-social person. We'll be investigating his possible link to the shootings of Agnieszka Preisner, Hutch Butler, Cindy Walker, Chantal Lee, and Martine Crawford. From our preliminary findings, it appears that Mr. Sackler killed himself. In fact, the evidence indicates he may have been playing Russian Roulette. All of the chambers in the gun he used were empty."

Despite the tragedy of the evening, entrepreneur Trent attempted to put a positive spin on the hotel's re-opening. "Everyone loves a juicy scandal. The hotel has stood for nearly seventy years. There's a lot of history here, and I think that will appeal to guests. Is the hotel haunted? I've said it before, and I'll say it again—I hope so! That will just add to Hotel Destiny's mystique!".

About the Author

Raymond Benson is the author of over forty books. His most recent novels of suspense are *Blues in the Dark*, *In the Hush of the Night*, and *The Secrets on Chicory Lane*. He is primarily known for the five novels in his best-selling serial, *The Black Stiletto*, as well as for being the third—and first American—author of continuation James Bond novels between 1996 and 2002, penning six worldwide best-selling original 007 thrillers and three film novelizations. Raymond's other novels include *Dark Side of the Morgue* (Shamus Award nominee for Best Paperback Original), *Torment—A Love Story*, and *Sweetie's Diamonds*, as well as several media tie-in works.

The author has taught courses in film history in New York and Illinois and currently presents ongoing lectures about movies with film critic Dann Gire. Raymond is also a gigging musician. He is an active member of International Thriller Writers Inc., Mystery Writers of America, the International Association of Media Tie-In Writers, and ASCAP. He served on the Board of Directors of The Ian Fleming Foundation for sixteen years. He is based in the Chicago area.

www.raymondbenson.com
www.theblackstiletto.net

BIBLIOGRAPHY

Novels

Evil Hours
Face Blind
Tom Clancy's Splinter Cell (as "David Michaels")
Tom Clancy's Splinter Cell—Operation Barracuda (as "David Michaels")
Sweetie's Diamonds
A Hard Day's Death
Metal Gear Solid (based on the videogame)
Dark Side of the Morgue
Metal Gear Solid 2—Sons of Liberty (based on the videogame)
Hunt Through Napoleon's Web (as "Gabriel Hunt")
Homefront—the Voice of Freedom (co-written with John Milius)
Artifact of Evil
Torment—A Love Story
Hitman: Damnation (based on the videogame series)
Dying Light—Nightmare Row (based on the videogame series)
The Secrets on Chicory Lane
In the Hush of the Night
Blues in the Dark

The Black Stiletto Saga

The Black Stiletto
The Black Stiletto: Black & White
The Black Stiletto: Stars & Stripes
The Black Stiletto: Secrets & Lies
The Black Stiletto: Endings & Beginnings
The Black Stiletto: The Complete Saga (anthology)

James Bond Novels

Zero Minus Ten
Tomorrow Never Dies (based on the screenplay)
The Facts of Death
High Time to Kill
The World is Not Enough (based on the screenplay)
DoubleShot
Never Dream of Dying
The Man with the Red Tattoo
Die Another Day (based on the screenplay)
The Union Trilogy (anthology)
Choice of Weapons (anthology)

Non-Fiction and Miscellany

The James Bond Bedside Companion
Jethro Tull—Pocket Essential
Thrillers—100 Must-Reads (contributor)
Tied-In: The Business, History, and Craft of Media Tie-In Writing
(contributor)
*Mystery Writers of America presents Ice Cold—Tales of Intrigue from the
Cold War* (co-editor, contributor)
12+1: Twelve Thrillers and a Play (anthology)

Curious about other Crossroad Press books?
Stop by our site:
http://www.crossroadpress.com
We offer quality writing
in digital, audio, and print formats.